the women of hearts book two

MARCI BOLDEN
BURNING
HEARTS

Cover design by Okay Creations
Book layout by Lori Colbeck

ISBN-13: 978-1-950348-26-8

the women of hearts book two

MARCI BOLDEN

BURNING HEARTS

PINK SAND
—— PRESS ——

PROLOGUE

THE SMOKE FILLING Wendi Carter's kitchen didn't surprise her. Even after taking a basic cooking course at her local grocery store, she could effortlessly burn water. What was astonishing was the fact that the smoke alarm wasn't wailing as she pulled the charred ground turkey off the stovetop. The recipe for Easy Taco Salad, a half page torn from a magazine, flittered to the floor in her rush across the room. She snatched the pan off the heating element and cursed the layer of meat stuck to the bottom.

In a routine she was far too familiar with, she dropped the pan into the sink, turned on the fan, and frantically waved her towel to disperse the smoke. Then she leaned back against the counter and looked up at the circle of plastic on her ceiling.

She was so acquainted with the screeching, she actually talked to the device in futile attempts to calm it down.

"Simmer down, Ol' Smokey" was what she usually said as she fanned away smoke from whatever she had burned. Then she'd climb on a chair, twist the plastic cover off the alarm, and pull the battery until the air cleared enough to not trigger the sensors.

This particular evening, however, Ol' Smokey was silent.

Which meant her culinary skills were so poor, she'd actually killed the detector's battery. She laughed as she considered just how many adults could claim that particular achievement.

After clearing the air, Wendi grabbed a new nine-volt battery from the overflowing junk drawer and climbed the chair she always used to reach the alarm. She twisted the cap off and removed the plastic covering. Staring at the innards, Wendi swallowed hard, trying to understand what she was seeing.

The battery wasn't dead. It was missing. In its place was a tiny device. One that, after a few moments of inspection, she identified as a wireless camera. She ogled the little contraption, confused how it could have gotten there. Just four days ago, as a blackened pizza cooled on her balcony, she had pulled the battery to stop Ol' Smokey from beeping. She'd replaced it after fanning out the kitchen.

The battery had been there four days ago. And now it wasn't. That didn't make sense. Wendi lived alone. She had a boyfriend, but he didn't have a key. No one had a key.

And no one had been in her house in the past four days.

At least not to her knowledge.

DESPITE HER MORNING ritual of practicing tai chi, Eva Thompson had little patience, especially for scumbags who put innocent people in unnecessary danger. The sweaty, borderline overweight man sitting across from her was doing just that. The president of the Jupiter Heights Condominium Association didn't seem to mind that the "events" he was describing were illegal activities that could lead to a serious incident. He was more concerned with making sure the reputation of the high-end residence remained unaffected.

A hidden camera? Inside someone's home? And this 1970s–era Ned Beatty–looking jackass had called HEARTS Investigative Services instead of the police why? Because he feared his fellow residents would panic. Of course they would panic. As well they should. A woman's privacy had been violated in her own home.

"The camera wasn't found in a common area, Mr.

Price, and you said she hadn't had any visitors or scheduled maintenance. That means someone broke into her home. This is a matter for the police." Eva stared him down, silently daring him to challenge her assessment.

He wiped his glistening forehead with the handkerchief he'd been clutching since sitting down. Normally she'd offer to turn the temperature down for a client in obvious discomfort. However, Neal Price deserved to be uncomfortable.

"Ms. Thompson, I assure you, if I believed our residents were in danger, I'd contact the proper authorities."

"I assure *you*, every woman in your building is in more danger than you can imagine. You have no idea of the intent the perpetrator had or how many other condos have been broken into, but let's assume it's just a little voyeurism directed at Wendi Carter. Just a little peep show he's after. What would have happened if she had caught him hiding the camera? Do you think he would have just smiled and waved as he walked out? She could have been hurt. If he is doing this in other condos, someone *could* get hurt."

He tightened his lips, and light reflected off the beads of sweat on his upper lip.

"What if his purpose was far more sinister?" she continued. "What if he was monitoring her, possibly still monitoring other residents, to determine the best time to rape and murder someone?"

Price huffed a breath out so hard his arched nostrils flared. "If you aren't interested in taking this case—"

"That's not what she's saying." Holly Austin, the lead agent at HEARTS, leaned forward. As little patience as Eva had, Holly had even less. Her hardened outlook on life had softened a bit after the last case she'd worked ended with her taking a bullet and landing a man in her bed, but she was still far from forgiving. Jack, her new boyfriend, hadn't exactly settled her, but having Holly get laid on a regular basis made everyone else's lives easier. She wasn't nearly as uptight today as she'd been even two months ago, but that didn't mean she'd tolerate this man's incompetence any more than Eva would. "She's simply pointing out that this situation may be more serious than you realize. Someone, potentially someone *within* your community, has broken several laws."

"Yes, Ms. Austin. I'm aware. That's why I'm here."

"Instead of making a police report," Eva pointed out.

Holly lifted her hand in the way that she did to shush someone. The movement, though simple, was imposing coming from Holly and usually had the intended effect. Eva stopped tossing accusations at the man, but she didn't stop glaring at him.

"Do you have the camera?" Holly asked. "The first images on the memory card should be the person who installed it."

He huffed as his shoulders sagged. "I can't find it. It was in my desk drawer, and when I went to get it before coming here, the camera was gone. I'll keep looking."

Eva ground her teeth so she didn't point out how utterly inept he had to be to lose vital evidence in a case.

Holly thought it, obviously, but she didn't say the words either. "Are there security cameras in other areas? Hallways, elevators, etcetera?"

"Yes."

Eva nodded. Okay. That was something. "Did you bring that footage?"

His cheeks darkened a few shades. "We contract our security out. The company provides minimal storage."

Holly creased her brow. She wasn't proficient in computer speak. Eva translated without pointing out what was probably Holly's only weakness.

"So," Eva said flatly, "they don't have enough storage to retain video?"

He nodded. "We only have about an hour or so before the old footage is lost."

"That must be a fairly basic package you're paying for," Eva said. "Have you considered upgrading?"

He stared her down. "I'm working on it."

Holly frowned. "Can you tell us more about the victim?"

He pushed a file across the table. Holly opened it, and Eva skimmed the first page. This association president suddenly seemed more like a prison warden. The page held the woman's photo, address, phone numbers, work information and, to top it all off, a record of every time she entered and left the secure parking lot using her key fob.

"This is everything a stalker could ever need. You know that, right?" Eva asked, not bothering to mask the allegation in her voice.

Price wiped his forehead again and then tugged at the collar of his white polo shirt. "There is extremely limited access to this information."

Eva cast Holly a glance, but Holly didn't turn her attention from the man. Holly was better at hiding her poker face than Eva. Joshua, the ex who Eva couldn't escape, used to tell her that she could at least *try* to hide her frustration. She couldn't then, and she couldn't now when he popped in and out of the HEARTS office as if he were one of the team members. Eva tolerated him because they did need him, even if she didn't like it. As the county coroner, he knew all kinds of nerdy science stuff that came in handy with the group of PIs.

She suspected by the apparent anxiety on Price's face when he glanced at her, licking the sweat off his flat upper lip, that he could see right through her, too.

"Only the association board and certain members of our property management team can access this." He flipped to another page in the folder. "Their names are here. I understand this is a serious situation, but if we call the police, we're going to scare whoever is doing this. Then we'll never find out who he is. There's a reason I reached out to you, Ms. Thompson. I want to catch him, but I don't want to scare everyone in the process. I suspect you can catch our perp discreetly."

She fought the urge to roll her eyes. His use of the term "our perp" made her want to snort.

"We are a close-knit community," he continued. "Everybody knows everybody in our building. The fact that we've been able to contain this as long as we have is a miracle. If this happens again, we *will* have to contact the police. As soon as they start snooping around, panic will spread. We want to keep this quiet, not just for the association but for our residents. We don't want people scared in their own homes. There is a vacant condo in the building. I'd like you to move in so you can integrate yourself into the community. Settle in and help us figure out who is doing this before it does get dangerous."

Eva sat back. "You can't afford that."

"I assure you, the association would rather pay you for this than pay for a marketing campaign to bounce back if this is exposed."

Holly glanced at Eva before saying, "You're talking twenty-four-seven surveillance. That's going to get expensive quickly."

"Well, if your agency is as good as you claim it to be, I don't expect this will drag on. I have a list of people who have access to the condos." He gestured to the folder as if to remind them. "Shouldn't be too hard for someone of your expertise to narrow it down. I *can* take my business elsewhere."

Eva slammed her hand on the folder before he could pull it away. "You need to understand that once we find out who has been doing this, you *will* have to notify the police."

Neal Price frowned. "Of course. We just want this to stop before it happens to someone else."

JOSH NEARLY DROPPED THE PIZZA, BREADSTICKS, TWO-liter of soda, and bagged salad he was balancing when the door of HEARTS swung open. The sweaty man barely glanced at him, as if Joshua were to blame for trying to enter as he was exiting. Despite the man's irritation, Josh was hoping he'd hold the door. "Could you just... Maybe..." His words faded as the man stormed off.

He watched, annoyed in his own right at the man's rudeness. But then the door opened again, and he was greeted by a warm smile from Sam, the receptionist-slash-assistant-slash-researcher-slash-gofer for HEARTS.

"Aw, Josh, are you bringing Eva lunch?"

He stuttered as he fought the overwhelming need to look away from her bright blue eyes. "Uh, no. *No*. Everybody. Me too. I was hungry." Heat started creeping up his neck as a surge of adrenaline caused his blood vessels to dilate. He'd integrated himself into HEARTS before he and Eva had started dating, and they'd agreed he'd remain a part of the team—even though she insisted he was an *asset* to the team, not a *part* of the team—after they amicably broke up. They hadn't even dated that long, just a few hot and steamy months before breaking up forty-three days ago. Not that he was counting...exactly. He was just good at remembering dates.

He didn't know why Sam always had to tease him about the short-lived relationship.

As the county coroner, he had a lot to offer the girls

—*women*. If he called them girls to their faces, he'd probably get his ass whipped. The *women* of HEARTS were strong and brave and intimidating as hell. But he admired each one of them.

Even Eva, despite her calling it quits for reasons he still didn't fully understand. He'd thought their relationship was going great. Though they often disagreed, they rarely fought. They had an amazing time together, always going on adventures and learning new things. And the sex? Josh didn't think he'd ever had sex as hot as he'd had with Eva, and she hadn't complained...at least not to him. The excuse she'd given him when she sat him down to tell him they couldn't see each other anymore was that he didn't believe in her abilities as a PI, and she couldn't date someone who didn't believe in her. No matter how much he tried to reassure her, she said they could be friends but nothing more.

Nothing he had said convinced her otherwise, so he was simply doing the best he could to stay a part of—*an asset to*—the team. These women were his friends now, people he had come to care about, and he didn't want them to turn on him because he and Eva hadn't worked out. If that meant bringing lunch once in a while to remind them he was worth more than an occasional scientific fact or unusual bit of information stored in his mind, then that was what he would do and had been doing for the last few weeks.

He slowed his pace as he neared the conference room where he always deposited the food he was offering—his ticket to remaining part of their tight-knit group.

"I don't like it," Holly said. "You shouldn't move into that place alone."

"You heard him," Eva replied, her tone softer but not lacking its usual clip. "The condo is one bedroom."

"So?"

"So?" Eva drawled.

"If one of us doesn't stay with you, you won't have any backup on site."

"He's not going to pay for two of us, Holly, and you can't expect someone to work for free."

"I don't mind," Holly said. "I'll stay with you."

"You're still recovering from a gunshot. How much backup do you think you'll be if something goes down?"

Josh stepped into the conference room, not speaking, not making his presence known, but he knew the moment Eva sensed his presence. Actually, she tilted her pert little nose up and inhaled before turning her face toward him... the pizza...and a brilliant smile broke the tension on her face.

"Lunch," she sang.

"What, uh, what's going on?" Josh asked Holly as Eva took the food from his hands. He knew better than to ask his ex. Since one of the things they'd fought about, the *only* thing they'd fought about, was the danger she put herself in working as private investigator, she'd stopped talking to him about work. Which had led to the imme- diate downhill slide of their relationship. He had seen enough bad things come through the morgue to know that Eva was in danger without choosing a high-risk profession. Murders were on the rise in the area, and women were far more likely to be the victims. Eva was already at risk. Dealing with criminals just heightened that.

"Stop," Eva ordered.

Josh blinked several times, jolted by her harsh tone. "What?"

"Obsessing about whatever morbid statistic your little brain is rolling around."

He opened his mouth to disagree, but he couldn't. Instead, he focused on Holly again.

She reached for a slice of pizza. "We have a new case."

"He doesn't need details," Eva muttered.

Thankfully, Holly wasn't as offended by his presence and continued. "Someone hid a spycam in a condo on the west side. The condo association president narrowed it down enough to think it was an inside job. He wants Eva to move in to integrate herself with the residents and find the sleazeball."

That familiar feeling washed over Josh. Another surge of adrenaline rushed through him, except this time his stomach spasmed. He wasn't embarrassed now. He was concerned. "You said you didn't want her to. You said it was dangerous."

"She didn't say that," Eva said.

Holly pushed the half-chewed food in her mouth to one side and said, "Not dangerous, per se, but it's a bit more risk than I'd like to take. She should have someone watching her back since she will be living this thing twenty-four-seven." She didn't have the best table manners. She didn't mind talking around whatever she was consuming any more than she minded licking away oozing condiments or grease from her fingers, which she did as soon as she was done speaking.

Eva, on the other hand, swallowed and wiped her mouth before speaking. Her manners were much better. "Don't encourage him. He already thinks I can't take care of myself."

Josh eyed Eva. Like he needed encouragement to consider her safety. If *she'd* considered her safety more often, maybe they wouldn't have had that fight that eventually led to them breaking up. She was so mad that he worried about her, but she never considered that he wouldn't have had to worry about her if she were more aware of the danger she put herself in sometimes. He'd spent the better part of their brief romance trying to convince her to let Holly or Rene take the more intense cases. They had military training. Sure, Eva had been a cop, but that was a long time ago. Besides that, it was natural for someone to become more relaxed as they became comfortable in their job. It was only a matter of time before Eva let her guard down and got hurt. Moving into a condo for any amount of time was just asking for her to get too comfortable.

If Holly was concerned, why the hell wasn't Eva? He understood her reasoning—it wasn't right for Holly to ask one of the other PIs to work overtime without compensation. And Eva was right. Holly was still recovering. She shouldn't overdo it or put herself at heightened risk.

"Me," he blurted without thinking. "I'll stay with her. I'll have her...six. Right? You call it her six?"

"We call it *cover*," Eva stated. "And I don't need you providing me cover. You are the least qualified person in this building, and I'm including Sam in that."

"Bite me, Thompson," the receptionist called from the other room.

Eva ignored her as she wiped her hands on a napkin and crossed her arms over her chest, staring Josh down with that cool gaze of hers. It wouldn't be so intimidating if her eyes weren't the color of Arctic ice against her porcelain skin. "Exactly what do you think you'd do if I found myself in trouble? Embalm someone?"

"Undertakers embalm corpses," he stated. "I examine them to determine cause of death."

She lifted her brows and tilted her pointed little chin as if that emphasized her point. Maybe it did. "You going to *examine* the bad guy, Josh?"

"A male presence is a deterrent to trouble," Holly said.

Eva darted her gaze across the table.

"That's just human nature, Eva," Holly said. "Men are naturally more intimidated by other men. Women tend to be seen as helpless victims. You know this." She focused on Josh. "You'd go about your life as normal, but you'd be living with Eva for a week, maybe longer. Are you up for that?"

The tension radiating off Eva was palpable. Her

condescending smirk disappeared as she tightened her jaw and stared—no, *glared*—across the table. "What part of one-bedroom condo are you not understanding, Holly? Where is he going to sleep?"

Holly shrugged. "Use your imagination."

Josh swallowed hard. He didn't need to use his imagination. He'd shared a bed with Eva enough times to know exactly what he was getting into.

Sitting back, Eva shook her head, causing light red curls to tumble around her shoulders. "No."

"Then we're dropping the case. You're not staying alone."

Eva's eyes widened. "No, we're not. Those women are in danger."

"Yes," Holly agreed. "And if I put you in that building without backup, you would be in danger as well."

"I can take care of myself," Eva stated through clenched teeth.

Josh shrank back in his chair. Uh-oh. Holly had inadvertently tripped Eva's trigger. Nothing set her off faster than the implication that she couldn't handle a situation. There were far too many police officers—and criminals—who had viewed Eva as inadequate when she was on the police force. The main reason she'd left the department and joined Holly at HEARTS was because she felt she had been passed up for promotions because of her gender and petite stature.

She might not be intimidating at a glance, but Josh

knew better, and the anger burning in her eyes would tell anyone else she wasn't to be messed with.

Holly, however, didn't seem put off by the obvious irritation she'd caused. She dropped her pizza and wiped her hands. "I'm not saying that you can't. I *know* you can. But living there means getting comfortable, and getting comfortable means unconsciously letting your guard down."

Josh was tempted to give her a high-five. He'd thought the very same.

Holly lifted her hand before Eva could speak. "I trust you. I know you are good at what you do. If I didn't, you wouldn't be here. But I am responsible for your safety, Eva. I will not put you in a position where you might inadvertently get lax and misstep. Someone will go with you."

Eva drew a slow breath before turning her attention to Josh, glaring at him as if this were his fault. He guessed it was, really. He'd volunteered, but he had no doubt Holly would have called the client and passed on the case if he hadn't.

Even so, Eva didn't appear at all appreciative. "Stay out of my way," she said coolly. "Let me do my job, Joshua."

"Fair enough," he said, already questioning whether Eva was right. Maybe this was a terrible idea.

[2]

Eva dropped her black duffle bag next to the navy blue sofa and put her hands on her hips. She scanned the furnished condo she'd call home for however long it took to find the resident pervert. The condo had an industrial design with exposed overhead silver pipes and concrete walls. Floor-to-ceiling windows had a reflective coating so she could see out but Peeping Toms couldn't see in. Funny how that probably made the residents feel safe.

The open-concept space was just under a thousand square feet in all but had plenty of places to hide cameras. She'd tucked the thermal camera from the office into her bag so she could scan for heat signatures emitted by any spycams that might already be discreetly placed in the condo.

If that were the case, consider the issue solved, since the first footage on hidden cameras tended to be of the person who hid them. The idiot would convict himself with his own footage.

Boom. Done. And she could get out of this disastrous situation before it even started.

"This is great," Josh said, coming to a stop beside her. "Look at how much natural light comes in here."

Eva closed her eyes. *Just breathe.*

Nope. That mantra still didn't help. Nor had yoga or an extra session of tai chi or beating the crap out of her Krav Maga instructor. She still wanted to strangle Holly for her ultimatum. Josh moved in, or HEARTS would drop the case. Eva had pointed out, several times, that having a male presence in the condo could detract from the residential voyeur's interest in her. Holly insisted that was a good thing. If he fixated on her and slipped cameras into her condo, he might realize she was an investigator, not just another victim. It was better if Eva didn't draw his attention.

Eva disagreed. She was trained to handle bad guys. She *should* have been drawing his interest. She shouldn't have been there just to investigate.

Josh bent to pick up her bag, but Eva swooped down and snagged the handles.

"I got it," she said.

He nodded. The man wasn't stupid. He had to sense her resentment at his intrusion. Not just having him in her space but having him *on* her case. He wasn't a private investigator. He didn't like private investigators. He'd told her over and over it was up to the police to solve *real* crimes.

She still didn't understand how he could have been surprised when she ended things between them. How could he expect her to date someone so blatantly opposed to her career choice?

Cutting in front of him, she carried her clothes and personal items into the one—*singular*—bedroom in the unit. "I get the bed."

Josh crossed the room and put his bag on the opposite side of the mattress from where she stood. "You get half of the bed."

A loud and sardonic laugh erupted from her. "No, Joshie. I get the *entire* bed. You get the couch."

His jaw muscles tensed. He *loathed* being called Joshie. Poking him with that particular stick felt incredibly good on an immature and petty level she should be above. She wasn't. He'd inserted himself into her life without her permission. She was going to make him regret it in every way possible. If that meant reaching all-time lows on the pettiness meter, she'd just have to make the sacrifice.

"We are supposed to be acting like a couple."

"Out there." She pointed toward the wall, indicating the building outside of the condo. "In here, we are nothing."

His lips pressed together. "This is a case of hidden cameras capturing people's every move. Don't you think it would be suspicious to the perp if he noticed we just moved in together but aren't sharing a bed?"

She planted her hands on her hips and rolled her eyes closed as she exhaled a slow breath. "First, I have no intentions of letting anyone sneak a camera into this condo. Second, the only people who actually say 'perp' are TV cops. Real cops, real investigators, do not use that term."

He tilted his head, clearly processing her statement. "What do you call them?"

"Suspects. Criminals. Pieces of shit. *Not* perps."

"Why not?"

Jerking her bag closer to her, she yanked at the zipper and directed her zinger straight at his soft spot: his love of *crime TV*. "Because we don't want to sound like dipshit fake cops scripted by Hollywood."

She carried an armload of neatly folded clothes to the closet. After hanging her blouses and slacks, she unpacked three pairs of soft-soled ankle boots and a pair of running shoes. When she finished, Josh shoved his way into the doorway and hung his clothes beside hers. She used the intimate area to her advantage and crowded him. She only came to his chin, but she narrowed her eyes, using the depth of her irritation to make up the size difference. Keeping her voice level but firm, she asked, "Do you remember what we talked about?"

"Y-Yes."

"If things get hairy, you get out of the way. Understand?"

"I understand."

"You are not trained to handle confrontation."

He frowned. "Just because you have a gun and do kung fu—"

"Krav Maga. There's a difference."

His shoulders heaved, and he puffed out his chest as he drew another deep breath. "I'm here to watch your back. Not get in the way. If there's trouble, I'll leave you to handle it."

"Good. First thing I need to do is document the area. I need pictures of everything so if something is moved or added, I'll notice when I do my daily inspection. Don't move anything without telling me. Got it?"

"I can help. Rene showed me what to look for."

Eva ground her teeth. Why couldn't her teammates just leave her to do this? Josh was an *asset*. He was *not* an investigator and had no business getting himself into possible danger. "No. You just...stay out of the way."

"Eva," he called before she could leave the room. "I thought we were okay after breaking up."

The sad puppy look in his eyes tugged at her heart, made her feel guilty for her show of resentment. She steeled herself against the temptation to cave and be nicer to him. She had put a wall between them for a reason. He'd broken her heart. And that hurt worse than any other injury she's ever experienced. Idiot.

Cocking her brow, she frowned. "Well, that was your second mistake."

His face sagged. "And the first?"

Instead of pointing out that his first misstep was getting involved with her at all, she snagged her camera and got to work. The faster she solved this case, the faster she could put some space between them.

JOSH DROPPED ONTO THE BED AND WATCHED EVA SNAP pictures of the bedroom, study all the lamps and clocks and pictures, and scan the room with her infrared camera. He didn't move until she moved on to the living area. Well, apparently they weren't okay. He hadn't realized that. Maybe someone with better social skills would have.

Eva wasn't exactly subtle. But he really wanted them to be okay, so he had forced himself into believing that they were...at least to some extent. She was right; he wasn't good at confrontation. And he wasn't good at recognizing when someone didn't like him. He worked with the dead for a reason; he sucked at understanding the living.

Chalk that up to geeky childhood scars. He'd always tried so hard, but it wasn't until he first met Holly that someone seemed to appreciate him for what he had to offer—and not just his knowledge. They had first met at a local law enforcement conference, but they'd had conversations about things outside of cadavers and biology and causes of death. When she'd introduced him to the rest of HEARTS, they had actually treated him with respect. He'd finally found a place where he felt he belonged.

He'd been especially taken with Eva. She was funny and sweet and considerate. When she wasn't so angry with him. They talked about the strangest things, things he never would have thought he'd be interested in. She shared the same innate curiosity he did, but she was drawn to areas he'd always shied away from.

She wanted to learn everything about rock climbing, guitar playing, sculpting. Her interests were all over the map, and every now and then they intersected with Josh's. Actually, he started actively intersecting them long before she noticed he was doing it.

Rock climbing? He lied and said he'd always wanted to try that. The truth was, when they walked up to an indoor wall the first time, he nearly vomited just looking at how high they were expected to climb. He'd swallowed his fear and climbed just as high, albeit quite a bit slower, than Eva. She'd patted his shoulder and smiled, and his heart nearly exploded. That was all the confirmation he needed. He could and would try whatever she asked him to.

Guitar? *Who doesn't want to learn to play the guitar?* he'd asked. In reality, he'd never even considered it. But sitting with her in a little indie music shop, her laughter ringing out as she clumsily strummed the strings, had made the effort worth it. Neither had ever perfected the instrument, and after a handful of lessons, she suggested they move on to something else.

Knife throwing? Um. Okay. Sure. He'd try that. He'd sucked at it, but seeing Eva's natural ability to hit a target had made him smile so much his cheeks hurt by the time they'd left the archery studio and grabbed chili dogs at a little mom-and-pop shop on the way back to town.

He never would have tried any of those things—including the hole-in-the-wall chili dogs—if he hadn't been tagging along with Eva. He should have heeded Alexa's warning when she pulled him aside one day and told him not to get involved with Eva. She said things wouldn't work out, that Eva was too strong for him. That wasn't exactly how she'd put it, but he'd understood her meaning. He'd convinced himself that they could overcome any differences they had. They'd spent so much time laughing and growing together. He'd thought they were stronger than they were.

He didn't even know things weren't working out until Eva had sat him down one night and told him she thought it was best to end things. He worried too much. That was her excuse. Of course, she called it "doubt." He *doubted* her too much. He didn't believe in her enough. Bull. Just because he let her know he was concerned for her safety didn't mean he didn't believe in her. Just because he wanted her to do something less risky didn't mean he doubted her.

He just didn't want to see her hurt. Why was that so wrong?

Josh's gaze landed on the clock. Remembering what Rene had taught him about spycam detection, he examined the face but didn't find a lens. Turning it over, he popped the bottom off and pulled out the batteries to search for an SD card or any other sign the clock could actually be a recording device. Sure, Eva had done that already, but it didn't hurt to double-check.

He was examining the device, tilting it from side to side, before a realization dawned on him. He was double-checking Eva's work. He was following behind her to make sure she hadn't missed something. Why would he do that? She was perfectly capable. He'd said that to her over and over when he'd been trying to convince her that he wasn't discounting her job as a PI. He trusted her. He believed in her. He never once doubted her.

But here he sat, following up on her work.

Shit. Maybe he *did* doubt her.

Reassembling the clock, he set it back on the night-stand and swiped his sweaty palms over his tan corduroys. He left the bedroom, stopping in the living room, where Eva was moving her camera over a lamp, looking for the distinct heat signature of a hidden camera. "I'm going to go check out the gym."

She stopped and looked over her shoulder, her brow raised in question.

He flexed his arms and imagined if he were in a cartoon, the muscles would jiggle before dropping down into an exaggerated anti-flex. "Never too late to start working out, is it?"

"Don't hurt yourself, Joshua. I'm not playing nurse-maid," she said before focusing on her job again.

Squeezing the keychain in his pocket to verify that he could let himself back into their temporary home, he left without another word. But as soon as the door shut behind him, he pulled his cell phone from his pocket. He scrolled through his contacts until he found Jack Tarek. Jack was

Holly's boyfriend and didn't seem to have a problem with her line of work. In fact, Jack, a police detective, seemed to appreciate her hardiness.

If he were ever going to get back on even ground with Eva, he needed to learn to accept, understand, and even *appreciate* the same attributes.

"Jack," he said when his call was answered on the third ring, "it's Joshua Simmons. I need your help. ASAP." Josh paused. "Do cops say ASAP?"

"Yeah, Joshua, we say that."

Josh nodded as he pushed the button for the elevator. Only then did he consider that he'd likely lose reception if he stepped inside the metal car. Why hadn't he waited to call Jack? Why hadn't he thought of that? Eva would have thought of that. Eva always thought two steps ahead of what Josh did. That frustrated him most days. He wasn't used to someone beating him to the obvious conclusion. Most of his life, he'd been the smartest person in the room, but more than once Eva had outsmarted him and shaken his confidence.

Was that the problem? Had she realized he wasn't as smart as he'd always presented himself to be?

"You okay, buddy?" Jack asked.

Josh looked around the crisp white hallway until he noticed a red sign indicating the staircase. He opened the door and stepped inside the echoing chamber. "Yeah. I'm good. Sure. How are you?"

"Good."

Suddenly nervous, Josh didn't know what to say. "You and Holly. You're doing okay?"

"Uh-huh," he drawled. "Unless you know something I don't."

Josh raked his fingers through his shaggy hair as he glanced around the stairwell.

"Joshua?"

"Huh?"

Jack was silent for a moment. "Do you know something I don't?"

He creased his brow. "No. Why?"

Another stretch of silence on the other end. "How can I help you?" Jack's voice was a bit more clipped than before.

"Um. Did Holly tell you I'm staying with Eva for a while? For a...you know." He glanced around, seeking any sign of a camera or microphone. The last thing he wanted to do was blow Eva's investigation by tipping off the perp...the bad guy...by talking about her case in a bugged stairwell.

"Yes. I think that's very nice of you. Holly was relieved that you agreed to look out for Eva."

"Well...Eva's pissed. I'm kind of scared to go to sleep."

Jack chuckled into the phone. "She can be a little frightening, but don't worry. She's too smart to kill you in a time or location where she would be the only suspect."

Josh sat on the top stair. "That doesn't help."

Jack outright laughed. "I'm not sure what you're after here."

Running his fingers through his hair, he stared at a clump of mud embedded in the stair tread. "How do you do it, Jack? How do you let Holly continue to do her job? Especially after she got hurt not that long ago."

"Well," Jack drawled, "the biggest thing to understand, Josh, is that I don't *let* Holly do anything. She's a full-grown woman who is perfectly capable of making her own decisions. So is Eva."

Joshua closed his eyes. "That came out wrong."

"I get it. I do. I'm used to being around strong women. I've worked with them for years. Holly's strength and bravery don't scare me, but I can see how you'd be unsettled by dating someone tougher than you."

"Well...I...I wouldn't say she's—"

"Josh. I don't have time to pussyfoot around. You want to hear this?"

He slumped. "Yes."

"Eva has spent a long time learning how to take care of herself. Not just physically but mentally. If she weren't capable of handling potential danger, she wouldn't be doing what she does."

"What if she gets hurt?" he asked, just above a whisper.

"You know, when all that stuff went down and Holly got shot, I was scared. I was terrified. The idea of losing her made my blood run cold. But she's not a porcelain doll that I can set on a shelf. I can't lock her in a room and tell her to stay. Even if she did listen—which she wouldn't—she'd be miserable and resent me for making her that way.

Yes, she puts herself in danger sometimes, but she does that to help people. To protect them. She wouldn't be Holly if she weren't trying to protect someone. And Eva wouldn't be Eva if she weren't doing the same. You know why she left the force. She didn't feel like she was taken seriously. She had the option to switch departments or join forces with Holly. She joined Holly because Holly believed in her abilities. You have to, as well. You love her, right?"

Josh didn't answer. He'd never said he loved her. Even when they were dating. He sure as hell wasn't going to say it now.

"You don't have to answer that," Jack said by way of saving him the struggle. "We all can see that you do. So... loving someone means wanting to see them happy. Eva is never going to be happy sitting on the sidelines. Accept that. Or don't. But if you don't, any chance you have to fix things will crash and burn before it gets off the ground. You have to trust that she can handle herself and that she knows what she's doing. Anything less is going to be treading on sensitive ground."

He opened his mouth. Closed it and then opened it again as nonsequential words bounced around his head. Finally he managed to put a sentence together. "I wasn't trying to get her back. I just don't want her to hate me."

"She doesn't hate you," Jack said, as if he knew exactly what was going on inside Eva's head. "If she hated you, she'd be indifferent to what you think about her. She's angry because she feels rejected by you. Women tend to feel rejected when men try to change them. So don't try to change her, Josh."

"I didn't—" His denial fell short. He had. He hadn't meant to, but more than once he'd suggested Eva only take research cases, lost-pet cases, or insurance-fraud cases while the other HEARTS handled the potentially more dangerous cases. He'd done that out of fear that someday she'd end up on his table at the morgue. Not because he didn't think she was smart, or brave, or capable. But naturally, that was how she'd taken it. "How do I fix this?"

Jack laughed softly. "That, my friend, is a question for someone else. Start with Alexa. She's the nice one."

"Ms. Thompson," Neal Price called as Eva left the community gym with a bag over her shoulder. Buried under the towel, shoes, and deodorant, Eva had a notebook, camera, and the thermal reader she'd used to search for hidden cameras in the common area.

She wasn't exactly disappointed that the ladies' locker room was clear of any spycams, but she was saddened to confirm that Wendi Carter had definitely been targeted. Eva's next step was to determine why so she could follow the breadcrumbs to who.

She glanced at the teenage girl lurking behind him and smiled sweetly. Her greeting was met with rolled eyes, so she returned her focus on the man who had hired her. "Good afternoon, Mr. Price."

"I trust you are finding your way around?"

"I am. The amenities here are wonderful."

He nodded slowly, eyeing her, clearly asking for more

information. She wasn't about to divulge anything, even in code, in public. Was the man an idiot? Did he want to announce to every resident in the building she was there to investigate a crime they didn't even know had occurred?

Instead of tipping her hand to anyone who could be eavesdropping, she widened her smile and waved in a half greeting to the girl behind him, making another attempt at breaking through the cloud of emo weighing her down. She simply stared, almost angrily, at Eva. The girl had the same tall forehead as Price and her dark, beady eyes mirrored his. Eva was confident in concluding this was his daughter. The lack of personality was a good hint as well.

Dropping her attempt at socializing with the angry teen, Eva focused on the association president again. "I saw a flier for a potluck in the community center?"

"We have a monthly get-together for the residents. When the weather is nicer, we cook out in the back area. If the weather doesn't agree, we use the community room. It's a nice way to stay neighborly."

"Great. Should I bring anything in particular?"

"Third floor residents bring a dessert."

"Perfect." She looked behind him again. "Will you be there, too?"

The girl scoffed, snorted, and rolled her eyes all in one unbecoming motion. "Only because I have to."

"Cody prefers video games and talking to strangers on the Internet over actual human interaction."

"Give it a rest," Cody muttered, storming by her father and Eva.

He sighed and lifted his hands as a sign of defeat. "Kids, huh?"

"Yeah."

Price closed the distance between them and lowered his voice. "Do you have time to meet me later?"

Eva tensed, his close proximity setting her on edge. Rolling her shoulders back only added an inch or so to her below-average height, but doing so significantly improved her ability to stare straight at him in a way that warned against attack on an unconscious level. "I don't have much to report just yet. Give me more time. I'll reach out to you."

He frowned.

"Mr. Price, I've been a resident here for all of four hours. Give me some time, please."

"Well, it didn't take you long to find the indoor pool and exercise facilities."

Cocking her brow to let him know she didn't appreciate the accusation, she said, "Or to confirm those areas are unaffected by your little problem."

Realization dawned in his eyes. He let his allegation fall without an apology, however.

She hadn't expected one. Price had already proven himself to be too proud to admit he could be wrong about anything. If he weren't, he would have realized the ridiculous approach he was taking to the *little problem* she'd mentioned. "Have you spoken with the security company to upgrade the memory storage for this building?"

"I'm working on it."

"Good."

He simply nodded. "We'll speak soon, then."

"Yup." She turned on her heels and focused on keeping her steps light instead of stomping as she was tempted to do. Jerk.

"He hits on everybody."

Eva stopped her march and looked to the shadows where Cody was slouched in an oversize chair, staring at her phone. "Excuse me?"

She glanced up, the same unamused stare on her face. "You aren't special. He hits on everybody."

"He wasn't—"

"Whatever." She pushed herself up and left the sitting area without another word.

"Wow," Eva muttered. Punching the button to summon the elevator, she silently thanked her lucky stars she didn't have to contend with one of those on a regular basis. She'd been a moody teen, too, no doubt. But somehow the emo-tech era of today's youth seemed a million times worse than the plain old-fashioned teen angst of generations past.

Inside the elevator, Eva looked up at the security camera. This particular recording device was intentionally placed to convey a false sense of security. If her instincts were right, somewhere in the building there were cameras recording unwitting females, violating their privacy in ways that would cause embarrassment and some level of trauma once discovered.

"I'm going to find you," she whispered to the unidentified asshole hiding those cameras. The elevator eased to a stop, and the doors slid open in a smooth and silent movement. None of the jerky motions most residential buildings had. Eva lived in an apartment, and her ride to the fourth floor was akin to one at an amusement park— loud, bumpy, and slightly malodourous from all the various people who crammed their bodies into the small space.

The elevator at Jupiter Heights was more like a sixty-second, first-class journey. Hard to believe someone who could afford to live in a building like this, surrounded by affluent professionals, couldn't control his voyeuristic intentions. Wasn't that why porn had been invented?

But Eva knew it wasn't about what he saw as much as how he saw it. The spying got him off. The outsmarting. The smugness of superiority. No worries, though. She'd knock the prick off his self-erected pedestal.

Opening the door to her new home, Eva immediately inhaled deeply. Something garlicky and spicy and...*Italian*...filled her nostrils, warmed her heart, and made her stomach growl. Joshua had a lot of natural talents, but the man was a living god in the kitchen. She eased her bag beside the sofa and toed off her tennis shoes. "Is that arrabbiata sauce?"

He smiled over his shoulder. "And ground sausage instead of meatballs."

She moved toward the kitchen. "Pasta?"

He nodded toward the ridged tubes of penne straining in the sink. "Of course."

"This just might work out after all," she said under her breath. "Need help with anything?"

"Set the table?"

She grabbed silverware from the fully stocked kitchen and then opened two cabinets before finding a stack of industrial-gray porcelain plates. The crackled glaze made them look intentionally aged and used. She didn't quite understand this design trend. Why buy something new because it looked old? Just go buy something from the consignment shop for half the cost.

She had to wonder who'd stocked the apartment for Neal Price. He'd gone to great lengths to fake her and Josh's residence at the condo, including a fabricated purchase agreement that Holly had insisted on. If the voyeur had inside access, finding out that Eva and Josh hadn't purchased the condo would be inevitable. A moving crew had brought in boxes and furniture to make it look like they were actually moving in. Someone had to have bought all this crap. Eva hadn't considered who that person was. She'd been too distracted by the man who would be occupying her space. She'd have to ask Neal who he'd worked with so she knew who else knew she wasn't a real resident.

Josh dumped her favorite sauce into a serving bowl. "Find anything in the common areas?"

"No." Returning to the kitchen, she checked the contents of the oven, and her mouth watered when she spied garlic bread, browned and crispy. If she didn't hate

Josh so much, she'd love him. Pasta with a loaf of perfectly toasted bread was her weakness. He knew this.

Suck-up.

With the cookie sheet of bread sitting on the stovetop, she swiped her finger into the remnants of sauce in the pan and licked it clean. Jesus. That was heaven.

"Good?" he asked, somehow materializing at her side.

She opened her eyes and moaned her approval as he dumped the pasta into a large bowl. He'd made plenty to have leftovers. If there was anything Eva loved more than a hot, steaming bowl of pasta covered in Josh's arrabbiata sauce, it was reheated pasta covered in Josh's arrabbiata sauce. Giving the chili peppers enough time to really do their thing made the sauce even better the next day.

Sitting at the table, she dropped a pile of penne on her plate, added far more sauce than needed so she'd have enough to scrape up with the bread, and dug in.

Josh's manners were a bit better. He took a smaller serving—he'd rather serve himself seconds than throw something away. Amateur.

She smirked at her assessment but didn't realize it until Josh pointed it out.

"I'm glad dinner made you happy," he said.

Glancing up at him, taking a moment to process his words, she let her smile widen. Mostly because she hadn't been grinning at what he'd assumed. "Thank you for dinner, Joshua."

"You're welcome, Eva."

She took a big bite and gave him a thumbs-up. "Delicious," she muttered.

He chuckled. "You're getting Holly's manners."

Eva snickered, too. She wiped her face on a napkin and rested her forearms on the edge of the table as she chewed. When she swallowed her mouthful, she said, "Delicious. I wasn't expecting dinner, so thank you. Really."

"I like cooking for you. You know that."

She lifted her gaze from the bread she was examining, her debate over which slice looked the most garlic-coated forgotten. She did know he liked cooking for her. She had liked cooking for him, too. Back before his conviction that she was a lousy investigator got to be too much for her to handle, they used to cook dinner together all the time. They'd be sure to make plenty so they could share their spoils with the HEARTS, which was much appreciated by the women. Most of them didn't cook for themselves. Alexa's abuela took care of her nutritional needs most days, and Rene preferred carryout, while Tika and Sam usually hit a bar and grill close by the office before heading to their respective homes. Now that Holly and Jack had made their hot little affair official, his mother Najwa tended to spoil them with delicious Egyptian dishes that the HEARTS were lucky enough to indulge in once in a while.

Eva's favorite meals had always been the ones she and Josh made together. They had made a great team. They'd worked in perfect unison in the kitchen—and other places, too. Sadly, he blew their unity into itty-bitty pieces by turning into an overbearing male. That wasn't the first time one of her relationships had hit the skids because of her line of work, but this particular crash and burn still stung.

"There's a potluck for the condo residents tomorrow," she said, intentionally changing the subject. "We are supposed to take a dessert."

His eyes lit with excitement. "Molten lava cake."

She furrowed her brows. "Maybe something less ambitious."

"Peanut-butter-and-jelly bars."

"No peanuts. Unless you plan on carrying EpiPens to avoid a lawsuit."

"Right." He centered his attention on stabbing pasta with the prongs of his fork. "Peach cobbler. Boring but safe."

Eva rolled her eyes. "Just how you like it."

Okay. This was awkward. Josh twitched his nose as Eva's long red hair tickled as he inhaled. She had warned him to stay on his side of the queen-size bed, threatening him with a litany of nonlethal wounds if he didn't. But she didn't say what the punishment would be for her rolling to *his* side of the bed.

Josh lay still, holding his breath so her strands didn't flutter around his face again. But that only lasted a few seconds before he exhaled and immediately inhaled again. This time, he had to move. Had to brush the irritant from his face. But he did so slowly, so as not to disturb her. Not because he was scared of her—which he kind of was, to be honest—but because he liked the way her cheek was pressed against his shoulder and her hand rested on his stomach as her light breath teased his sparse chest hair. Even if her hair was torturing him.

Lightly brushing the instigating hairs from his nose, he slid his hand lower, daring to cradle her head in his palm. Then, as if of their own volition, his fingers curled into the messy bun she always pulled the reddish-blond mass into before bed. How many times had he held her like that as their bodies moved together under the blankets? How many times had he gripped her hair and pulled her against him so he could deepen a kiss?

Countless.

They hadn't dated for years or a lifetime, but they'd been together long enough for him to know that he missed the intimacy they'd shared. Not the sex. *Okay*. Not *just* the sex. They had shared a deeper connection from the day they'd met. Sparks had been immediate, at least on his part. The first time she'd kissed him after a knife-throwing lesson, breath spicy and tongue tasting like chili from the dog she'd just finished, his body had sprung to life. Her kiss had turned him into a starving wolf on the hunt. He'd never been aggressive, but he'd been starved for her, and that moment had turned from sweet to heated in seconds.

In an instant, they'd gone from friends hanging out to

passionate lovers. All the excitement she'd shown rock climbing, and the silliness during their guitar lessons, and the natural grace when throwing knives had come together as she'd pulled him into her apartment and straight to her bed. They'd moved together in a harmony he'd never had with anyone else. They were connected in a way that he'd never been with anyone else.

God, he missed that. He missed her. He missed *them*. Wrapping his arm around her, he pulled her tighter against him. He smiled as she wriggled a bit closer.

Staring at the silver-blue shadows dancing across the ceiling, Josh considered the conversation he'd had with Alexa while cooking dinner. Jack had been right, as always. Alexa was the "nice" one of the HEARTS. Not that the rest of his friends weren't; they just didn't have the sisterly affection and patience Alexa did. All the women were laser-focused, which didn't always allow for time to sit down and nurture his wounded soul.

Alexa, however, had listened as he explained that he didn't think Eva was weak; he was simply concerned for her safety and wanted her to avoid unnecessary risk. She sympathized with his concerns, as she tended to do, and then gave him a firm slap of reality, not the "Eva can take care of herself" lecture he was expecting. She understood that his mind didn't work in shallow reassurances. He was too analytical.

Instead, she broke down Eva's training: a brown belt in Krav Maga required years of training with thousands of hours of learning techniques to protect herself, and she was a highly trained gun-owner as well—not to mention that she'd spent seven years as a beat cop before joining Holly and the other women to form HEARTS.

Then she hit him with the zinger.

Eva might be in more risky situations from day to day than other women, but she was aware of that. That awareness heightened her senses, making her far less likely to become a victim of crime or violence than the everyday woman who buried her head in her phone as she walked along, assuming nothing bad would ever happen. Eva wasn't foolish or careless. She was smart and capable.

Joshua was being paranoid. He always had been. He always saw the worst in every person and situation. He'd grown up being the outcast, the black sheep, seeing the uglier side of people, and felt the need to protect Eva from the hurt he knew existed in the world. But that was silly. She was perfectly aware of the hurt people could cause. She'd been dealing with it a long time, too.

Even so, he pulled her closer. He couldn't imagine what he'd do if anything ever happened to her. He'd be lost. Broken. Holding her hair in his fist, he closed his eyes and inhaled, committing her scent and heat and feel to his memory, wishing he could somehow shield her from the monsters they both knew hid in the shadows.

[4]

EVA LISTENED INTENTLY while the woman on the other side of the table told her all about how their neighbor, Shane Tremant, was well known for being the building perv and that she would do well to avoid him.

"If he comes into the pool while you're there, just skedaddle. Don't even try to avoid him. That's pointless," Melly said. She rolled her gray eyes. "He'll be on you like a fly on honey. Trust me. I know. He *accidentally* grabbed my ass in the pool one day." Her air quotes were paired with another roll of her eyes.

"How do you know it wasn't an accident?" Eva pushed.

Melly pressed her plum-tinted lips together. Eva was tempted to ask what kind of lipstick she used that could hold up to the hot dog and baked beans she'd eaten but didn't want to distract her. "Because," she said, "if it'd been an accident, he wouldn't have squeezed."

"No." Eva took a breath to calm her fury. "He wouldn't have." Glancing toward the man in question, she caught him watching her. His intent stare, though unsettling, wasn't what captured Eva's attention. The oversize car key fob he held was of much more interest. He wasn't toying with it in some nervous twitch. He held the fob deliberately, as if...aiming it at her and the other two women who had been hovering over the dessert table for the last ten minutes.

Eva wasn't about to give Josh an ego stroke, but none of the other desserts she'd sampled came close to his. She'd been using tongs to add a strawberry cheesecake mini muffin to her plate when Courtney and Melly had introduced themselves. They'd easily fallen into conversation about the sweet offerings before moving into a round of neighborly chatter. With Eva being new to the community, Melly felt it was their duty to warn her about some issues, and Eva was all ears, gently nudging for more information. Courtney nodded in agreement occasionally but tended to smile and bat her overly made-up eyes more than contribute verbally.

Nothing was more valuable to a PI than a nosy neighbor with a taste for gossip, so Eva aimed most of her questions at Melly.

While forcing a bright smile in the general direction of Shane Tremant, she kept her focus on his hand. Why did he have a car key at the community potluck? He wasn't acting like he had someplace else to be. And who handled their keys like that? With such deliberate intent. That was suspicious as hell.

Cameras could be hidden in all sorts of everyday things, including fake car key fobs like the one he was holding. She'd have to try to get her hands on that thing and examine it. She was eyeing the fob when she lifted her gaze, and Shane smirked at her, clearly taking her interest in his potential criminal behavior as something else. His smile sent a jolt through Eva. She'd met a lot of creeps in her time, but she usually wasn't affected by them. Something sinister lurked behind that man's smile and instantly landed him on her radar.

She'd keep an extra-special eye on that asshole, only not in the way he apparently hoped.

"His wife is insane, and she *will* blame you if she catches him," Melly said, pulling Eva's attention back to her. "And once Tiffany gets on your case, she's harder to get rid of than her perverted husband."

"Did you report the assault to management?" Eva asked.

Melly creased her brows. "The assault? Oh, you mean that jackass grabbing me? No. Our homeowner's association is basically a popularity contest. Shane got pretty much the entire board elected."

Courtney agreed. "The only thing that sleazeball Neal Price has going for him is that Shane is his best friend."

Eva scanned the crowd until she found Price, the man who had hired her. He was standing next to a stiff brunette who had a smile stuck to her face. Well-practiced, no doubt, in the art of socializing, the woman elbowed the teen next to her until Cody stopped chewing her nails. Unlike the other day, Cody now wore shorts and a T-shirt. Both were black, but at least she appeared somewhat dressed for the occasion instead of for a skateboarder's funeral. She, however, didn't have the woman's—Eva presumed her to be Cody's mother—plastic smile.

While at the HEARTS office, Price had said only a few people had access to the tenants' private information. Shane Tremant's name was not on that list, but maybe Price had chosen to omit it. Or maybe he foolishly trusted his BFF to not be a creepy sexual predator. Not to mention that if Tremant was a trusted confidant, he could have easily stolen information from Price without his knowledge.

But that didn't *feel* right to Eva. She had a nagging suspicion that if one of those men were guilty, they both were guilty. If she'd learned one thing as an investigator, it was to trust those gut checks. She believed what these women were telling her, mostly because her initial impression of Neal Price was that he was a self-centered prick, but also because Shane Tremant put off an air of arrogance that was often found in sexual predators. Men like that could sweet-talk the panties off an eighty-year-old nun.

"Neal is pretty much worthless," Courtney continued. "If you have an issue, it's best to handle it on your own. He's only in the role of president for show."

"Good to know," Eva said, scooping a larger than

necessary helping of Josh's peach cobbler onto her plate.

"This is delicious," Courtney moaned. "Your boyfriend made this?"

Eva smiled, biting off the initial reaction to point out that Josh was *not* her boyfriend. "He sure did."

"Does he cook a lot?"

"Yeah. We both do, but Josh is better at it," she said honestly.

"You are so lucky," Melly offered. "My boyfriend doesn't lift a finger."

"I don't know why you put up with him," Courtney stated. "Single is better. By far."

Eva glanced at Shane Tremant as the other two women debated the pros and cons of their respective relationship statuses. He was still watching them. Clearly something was rolling through his mind. His stare was piercing, his attention unwavering. Eva's gut turned as he continued his scrutiny. Most voyeurs weren't so blatant, but something about him was off, which sent him right to the top of Eva's short list of suspects. Short list being *one* at the moment.

Shane Tremant. She cemented his name to her memory so she could do a background check as soon as she and Josh got back to their condo.

"I got this," Josh muttered under his breath as he glanced around the men's locker room. Rene had taught him what to look for when detecting spycams, and Eva had reinforced it a dozen times because she thought he was an idiot. Trying to act casual, he took much longer than necessary to tie his shoes, waiting for one of his neighbors to finish dressing and leave him alone. Two seconds. Eva told him over and over, he just needed two seconds. He'd know that quickly if the key fob Shane loved to hold so much was a camera.

Look for a lens or a USB port.

Eva had said that over and over, too. Her lack of faith in him was frustrating as hell. But well deserved. He got what he gave. However, he was working to change that. He'd done what Alexa had suggested and stood back, asking questions instead of going with his usual approach of trying to tell Eva how much he knew about whatever she was investigating. In his own defense, he kind of did that with everyone. Not just Eva. The curse of having an IQ of one thirty-nine was that he usually did know more than everyone else, and he wasn't always the best at sharing his knowledge in a way that wasn't condescending.

He was working on that, too.

Right now, though, he had to focus on inconspicuously picking up that fob and examining it without getting caught.

Stretching as he stood, he paced back and forth, looking around him. On his third pass by the fob sitting on the bench, he scooped it up and looked at the edge—all four sides—but found no indicator of a lens. Pushing the button on the top left corner, he released the metal key and examined the space behind where it had been tucked inside the black plastic. Nothing. No sign of ports or a memory card or anything else that could be construed as suspicions. This was a key. Just a key.

"Gonna steal my car?"

Josh nearly dropped the fob. Feeling that damn adrenaline rush, he held the pocketknife-sized gadget up and forced a dumbfounded look to his face. "I've never seen something like this."

Shane screwed up his face in a way that let Josh know he didn't believe him, one brow arched as he narrowed his eyes and held his hand out. "Really? These are pretty common nowadays."

"Uh... I drive...an old...Ford." He stuttered out the words before dropping the fob into Shane's giant palm. His hands were big enough that he could probably grab Josh by the head and toss him into a locker without much effort.

"What kind?"

Oh. Shit. Josh might be one percentage point away from joining Mensa, but that intelligence did *not* spread to motor vehicles. "Mustang." He'd heard Jack and Rene talking about those before. She owned one that Jack had drooled over at one of the many get-togethers HEARTS had invited Josh to.

"Year?"

"Sixty-eight."

Eva had coached him to keep his lies, if he had to

cover his ass like he was doing now, tied to truths so he could remember them. Rene's car was a '68.

"Cool. Take me for a ride sometime?"

Rene would cut his tongue out if he even suggested it. "Sure thing."

Shane's monster hand landed on Josh's shoulder as the man started for the door. "Enjoy your workout."

Pumping his fist in the air like he'd witnessed other men do, he said, "Yup. Will do. Take it easy, Shane." Once alone, Josh exhaled and sat on the bench as the surge of chemicals in his bloodstream leveled and his muscles started to quiver.

Eva did this crap for a living? Sneaking and lying and confronting? *Gah.* No thanks. He'd take working with the dead any day.

Grabbing his bag, he left the locker room, looking as casual as he could, despite his hands and knees trembling from the fight-or-flight response he'd just experienced. In the elevator, he leaned back and closed his eyes, finally releasing some of the anxiety coursing through him. He wondered if Eva had these same reactions when staring down a potential bad guy.

Well, of course she did. That was exactly how the human body—*any* human body—responded. Even those that belonged to the HEARTS. They had just been trained to deal with the surge so it didn't control them. They controlled it. Just like Alexa told him. Eva had spent years training how to properly respond in moments just like that one.

She always seemed so in command of her body and emotions. On some level, he'd attributed her cool-as-a-cucumber demeanor to being a little bit cocky about her role as a PI, but now he suspected there was more to it. She was in control, always aware of her body and emotions, because losing control was a hazard in her line of work. If he'd stumbled any more than he had in front of Shane, the man probably would have suspected something was off about Josh. Suspicion could ruin Eva's case.

Josh took a deep breath and moved through one of the tai chi poses he'd witnessed Eva do a hundred times before. He needed to have better control, quicker responses, so he didn't draw attention to himself or Eva. He made a mental note to look into a studio to take classes. He'd like to have more regulation of his adrenaline rushes, too.

Straightening up as the doors slid open, he took long steps toward the condo. Not running but certainly not walking either. He was eager to tell Eva what he'd found, or rather *hadn't* found, in the key fob to see what their next step should be.

"Well?" she demanded as soon as he closed the door behind him.

He shook his head. "Nothing. It was just a key."

She narrowed her eyes a bit, as if she weren't sure she believed him. "You looked for a lens?"

"Yes."

"And you opened it to see if there were ports or an SD card?"

"Yes. There was nothing. Just a key."

She dropped into a chair at the dining table so hard the square feet skidded an inch or two against the highly polished cement floor. "Damn it. I was so sure."

"What about you?" He set his bag next to the sofa and headed for the papers she'd spread across the table. "Finding anything in the background checks on Price and Tremant?"

She flipped her notebook shut before he could reach her and started gathering papers and photos. "Not much. Not yet, anyway. I'm still digging."

Josh didn't mean to look so hurt, but he actually felt his face sag as she hid her work from him. He stopped closing in on her and stared, not knowing what to say after her obvious display of shutting him out.

A loud sigh escaped her full lips. "Sorry. Habit."

It was a habit she'd started when they were dating. She hadn't minded talking about her work with him until he'd started pushing back with questions about danger and security. After that, she'd start closing her files, exiting out of windows on her laptop, and changing the subject when he walked into the room.

He'd really screwed up.

"You're not an investigator, Josh," she said, as if that explained her response. "I shouldn't have asked for your help with the key fob. That was giving you mixed signals. I'm sorry."

"I don't mind helping." Finishing the trek he'd started, he sat at the table. "I *want* to help."

She met his gaze, but he couldn't read her response. He'd never been able to read people like she could. She would have had to send smoke signals and plaster pictures on a billboard before he understood what looked to be sadness in her eyes.

He was tempted to ask what she was thinking, but instead of pushing, he rolled his shoulders back and shared the decision he'd made. "I thought I'd start doing tai chi. Can you recommend a place?"

Her eyes changed, but this time the message was clear. Confusion. Her morning ritual was the one thing she was interested in that he just hadn't wanted to try with her. He had been intimidated by the movements and hadn't really believed the power of calm she said the practice brought. Only after dating her for some time had he started to change his mind, but they had moved on to learning other things. "Really?"

"Yeah." He laughed uneasily. "Down in the locker room, Tremant almost busted me."

She lifted her brows. "Are you okay?"

"I started shaking so bad, I could hardly hide it. I'd like to learn how to keep my cool. You always said tai chi helped control your stress, so..."

"And you always said tai chi was boring."

"Well..." Okay, he had said that. "I've changed my mind. I'd like to take some classes and learn more."

The stress between them seemed to ease as she smiled. "Yeah. Okay. I can set you up."

"Think you could show me a few moves in the meantime?"

Eva stared at him for a few moments before standing. "Help me move the coffee table. I don't want you to hurt yourself."

Once they had enough space, she ran her hands down his arms. Josh swallowed hard when her touch caused his hormones to amp up as his body confused the situation and automatically started preparing for sex. Another situation he'd like to help control. On an instinctual level that he couldn't suppress, his body recognized Eva as a potential mate. Just being near her made his levels of reproductive hormones increase.

He took a breath as he imagined her frowning and demanding he speak in layman's terms.

Horny.

Being this close to Eva made him horny, and he couldn't help it. And having her stroke her hands down his arms was an automatic signal to his body that he should prepare to mount and breed her.

"Josh," she stated firmly in his ear.

"Huh?"

She peered up at him. "Are you okay?"

"Yup," he said, ignoring the way her vanilla scent wafted up to him and made him want to snatch her up and carry her to the bedroom. He could, too. He'd done it before. Scooped her tiny frame up into his arms as if she weighed nothing as he rushed to his bedroom. He'd tossed her down, and they'd rolled around, laughing and teasing as they pulled at each other's clothes. Then they'd made love so fierce his neighbor had banged on the wall and told them to knock it off.

"Feet shoulder-width apart, or you're going to fall on your ass," she warned, reminding him that they'd been in the middle of something before his mind had wandered.

Oh. Right. Tai chi. Standing beside him, she mimicked the pose. Moving her arms in a circle, she pressed her palms together and brought them to her chest as she gracefully bent her knees.

"Rise as you breathe in," she said in a soft, soothing tone he rarely heard from her. "Sink as you breathe out."

He tried to focus on doing as she said, but damned her velvety voice. She touched him, her palm against his back as the other pressed to his upper chest, and he had to swallow hard yet again.

"Don't bend. All the movement is in your arms and knees." She eased her hold, stepping back, and he wanted to lean forward again just so she'd correct him. "Rise," she said. "Sink."

He did the move several times.

"Nice. Want to try something a bit more difficult?"

"I could barely nail down bending my knees."

She laughed but didn't heed his warning. "Try this."

With a grace Josh had never possessed, Eva smoothly swung her arms and stretched out one leg, then brought them both to center, lifting her knee chest-high.

"I can't do that," he insisted.

"You can. Watch." She did the same move with the other leg. "Now you try."

Josh planted his feet, moved his arms, and then lifted his knee. And immediately started toppling over. Eva pressed her hands to his arm, laughing as she steadied him. His heart lifted as, for just a moment, he was transported back to how they used to be. Fun. Relaxed. Silly. Easygoing.

Perfect.

"You have to move in time with your breath so your core keeps you balanced. Try again." This time she stood close, helping him move slowly, encouraging him to take a long, deep breath and then let it out slowly. "Nice," she whispered when he finished the posture without falling over.

Planting his feet on the floor, he smiled down at her. He liked having her so close he could feel her body heat escaping her and smell the scent of the shampoo she used to keep the sheen of her hair from dulling against the chemically treated city water. Once again, Josh was tempted to pull her closer, but she took a big step back, saving them both from his primal need.

"Okay," she said, spreading her feet far apart. "Try this one."

She put him through several more postures before declaring he had enough to get started on cultivating his life energy. Moving into the kitchen, she pulled out a whole chicken and set it on the counter. "I thought we'd try chimichurri roast chicken tonight."

"Sounds good. Want help?"

"Wash and cut the veggies?" she asked, pulling a paper bag with a local grocer's logo from the fridge.

Inside he found rainbow carrots and baby potatoes of various colors along with some onions and other fresh ingredients. "So what's next in your case?"

She seemed hesitant to answer, focusing on rinsing the chicken. "There's something about Shane Tremant I don't like. Just because his key wasn't a camera doesn't take him off my list. Melly, the woman from the dessert table, doesn't have a very high opinion of his wife, either. I'd like to get my own read on her."

"And Courtney?"

"She didn't have too much to say about the Tremants, but she certainly doesn't like Neal Price. She says he's worthless and the only reason he is president of the HOA is because Shane convinced people to vote for him. She said if we have any issues, it's best to deal with them on our own."

"That actually seems pretty typical of how HOAs work, doesn't it?"

She chuckled as she put the chicken on a sheet pan. "Hand me the olive oil, please." He did, and she drizzled it over the skin.

"What should I do now?"

She nodded toward her phone. "Check the recipe."

Flipping her phone over, he smiled at the background image. Still a picture of the two of them. She'd taken the shot after they'd gorged on what a local magazine had dubbed the area's best hamburgers. They were full and content and had smiled brightly as she leaned back against his chest and angled the camera to get the restaurant's sign standing proudly behind them. He fucking loved that picture. Seeing it now made his heart ache.

"Find it?" she asked.

He tapped on the browser icon, and it opened to the recipe. "Yup. I need to cut the carrots lengthwise, and you get to find the food processor to make the chimichurri sauce."

She scoffed. "I thought you were making the sauce."

"I'm pouring the wine."

She glanced back as he grabbed a chilled bottle of sauvignon blanc and two glasses. "Fair enough."

Josh focused on twisting the corkscrew into the bottle as he watched her bending to peer into cabinet after cabinet before pulling out the food processor. After pouring the wine, he leaned back, content to soak in the normalcy surrounding them.

5

Eva sat in her inconspicuous black sedan for seventy-five minutes before Tiffany Tremant left the spa, looking no more or less perfect than she had walking in. This was one seriously pampered housewife. Before the spa, she'd sat with a group of women sipping coffee in an upscale chain coffeehouse. They'd then perused several boutiques before parting ways, pecking each other's cheeks like perfectly primped hens. Eva was waiting for her chance to pounce on Tiffany alone, but the woman had disappeared into one of those strange and frightening places that did manis, pedis, and other overly feminine things.

Eva avoided those with everything she had. She didn't mind painting her nails or wearing makeup if needed, but she certainly didn't go out of her way to look cutesy. She saved that for Tika and Sam. Once a month, the HEARTS spent a Saturday together just to bond as a team. No matter what event they planned—just lunch or training at the firing range—Tika and Sam always ended the day with manis and pedis. They invited the rest of the group, but other than Alexa, who occasionally decided to get her stubby nails painted, no one else ever took them up on their offer.

Tiffany walked several stores down, in the opposite direction from where she'd parked her car, so Eva didn't pull hers from the curb. Instead she made a note in her book and pressed the button on her cell phone to activate the walkie-talkie app. "She's headed down the street. I'm following on foot."

"Check in in five," Holly replied over the phone.

"Yes, ma'am," Eva said, pushing her car door open. She stepped out into the sun as a breeze whipped her long hair around her. She wanted to pull the mass back into a messy bun to keep it from her face, but the shops where Tiffany Tremant was spending her time and money didn't really support the don't-give-a-fuck style.

Following her into a little boutique, she scanned the room, spotting her in the lingerie section holding up a bright red bra and panty set. Eva immediately flashed the image of Shane Tremant licking his lips with excitement. Her stomach rolled. Violently.

A shudder rolled through her, and she made a face. *Yuck.*

She forced the vision from her mind and scanned the clothing with feigned interest. She smiled and turned down the offer for help from an overly attentive worker as she made her way toward where Tiffany was now holding up a black slip of a nightgown. Clearly that was *not* intended for sleeping.

Mrs. Tremant had seduction on her mind. Eva had to wonder if her intended target was her husband after all. But she wasn't undercover to catch an adulteress in action. She was there to catch a voyeur, and this woman's husband was high on her list. She didn't care whom Tiffany slept with. She cared about getting more insight into the inner workings of the Jupiter Heights Condominium Unit Association.

She glanced up, as if seeing Tiffany for the first time, and plastered a bright smile on her face. "Hi," she cooed in the way fake perky women tended to do. She snapped her fingers and rolled her eyes, pretending to think. "Oh, shoot. I'm *so* bad with names."

Easing the satin and lace back onto the rack, Tiffany put her sorority sister mask firmly in place—the forced smile that seemed far too perfect. Pressing freshly manicured fingertips to her chest, landing on a trio of thin gold chains in varying lengths, she batted her false eyelashes. Apparently nothing about this woman was real. "Tiffany Tremant. You're Eva, right?"

"I am." She held her hand out, but Tiffany waved as if to dismiss the greeting and wrapped her fingers lightly around Eva's shoulders, pressing their cheeks together and smacking an air kiss loudly in her ear.

"We're Jupiter Heights family now," she purred as she leaned back. Her smile spread even more, and she batted her eyelashes even faster. "Family doesn't shake hands."

Eva giggled. "How nice."

"You're new to the area, right? I think that's what Neal told Shane."

Eva blinked her own eyes, as if connecting dots in her head. Of course she knew who Neal and Shane were, but she wasn't about to let on. "Oh, *Neal Price*." She giggled again. "Sorry. Like I said, I'm bad with names." She made a show of creasing her brow. "Did I meet Shane?"

"My husband." Tiffany put her hand on Eva's. "Big guy. You were staring at him during the potluck the other day."

Eva bulged her eyes in a genuine show of shock. People didn't often surprise her, but Tiffany's blatant accusation did. "I was?"

There was a hint of malice in Tiffany's eyes, but she quickly covered it. "According to him. Then again, he thinks everyone is staring at him."

An uncomfortable laugh left Eva. Melly hadn't been kidding about Tiffany Tremant. Something odd flickered behind the social-butterfly facade. Curiosity, perhaps. Was she testing to see if Eva would confess to being interested in her husband? "Why would people stare at him? If you don't mind my asking."

She seemed to relax a bit. "They're not, but he thinks the world is in love with him. Have you ever shopped here before?"

"No. I was just browsing, really."

"Nonsense." She skimmed over Eva's basic black suit.

As a PI, she needed to blend in. Everything she and

her team did was right down the middle. Straight medi-ocre. No wild clothes. No crazy hairdos. Blending in was their intention. Eva did that well. Tiffany Tremant clearly didn't approve.

"You need...a few *new* things." She wriggled her fingers in the air as if summoning a pack of perfectly coifed French poodles. Funnily enough, several salesgirls came running, practically tripping over themselves to get to her first.

Tiffany was almost a foot taller than Eva and easily draped her arm over Eva's shoulder as she steered her toward the back of the store. "It's obvious you like more neutral colors, but Eve"—apparently the *uh* syllable was too much work?—"we need to incorporate some color into your world. Do you work, or..." She trailed the words off and batted her eyes.

"I'm a librarian." That was the backstory she and HEARTS had concocted, and she felt fairly confident it was a safe one. Few people seemed to know that libraries still existed, let alone wanted to have a long discussion about what being a librarian entailed.

Tiffany's brow almost creased, but the tight skin fought to remain in place. "How can you possibly afford a condo at Jupiter Heights?"

Ugh. Smug bitch. "My boyfriend is a doctor."

She puckered her lips and made a cooing sound like she'd just heard the most adorable thing. "Oh, honey, you should marry him before he gets away."

Eva simply smiled. Wow. She'd thought women like that only existed in novels. "And you?"

She giggled. "My job is supporting my husband in his endeavors so he can be as successful as possible. This"— she gestured around the boutique—"is where I buy my uniforms. Socializing is my specialty. I don't want to brag"—however, she was clearly going to—"but I made him the man he is. He owns two car dealerships, several rental properties, and recently ventured into home security."

Home security? That was interesting, considering he was so tight with Neal Price, who admitted to having shit for security at the condo he was so desperately trying to preserve.

Eva smiled and blinked rapidly. "Home security? You mean like door alarms or cameras or what?"

She rolled her eyes. "Oh, I don't listen to any of that. I just make certain he knows the right people, attends the right events, and dresses the right way. Which brings me back to you."

"Me?"

Pinching her fingers together, she creased her brow, clearly working against a strong dose of Botox. "You have lovely features and beautiful hair. Just a bit more effort in your appearance would make all the difference." Lifting Eva's strands, she *tsked*. "Next stop, my beautician. Someone needs a trim. Trust me, Eve, you don't want a man who puts you in a condo at Jupiter Heights to get away." Her eyes took a bit of a hard edge. "You must be careful. There are always women trying to snag a man like that. Even if he *is* taken."

Eva put on an air of sad innocence, but she saw a glimpse of what Courtney and Melly had warned her about at the potluck. Tiffany Tremant was very possessive of her husband. Not because of her husband but because he was her ticket to the lifestyle she wanted to remain accustomed to.

Tiffany called to the salesgirls to bring in some clothes for Eva to try, the touch of a threat in her gaze gone as quickly as it had appeared. As soon as she was alone, Eva tapped out a text to Holly.

Checking in from boutique hell. If you don't hear from me in an hour, bring me an oversize sweater and some Chucks.

Holly immediately responded. *Who's Chuck?*

Eva rolled her eyes. *Never mind, Hol.*

She tucked her phone into her pocket just as the door opened and a rack was pushed in. A rack. As in a metal frame filled with outfits. Eva's smile was as fake and frozen as Tiffany's had been during the potluck. "Wow. That's...a *lot* of clothes."

Tiffany barely seemed to be able to contain her excitement. For the first time, her smile looked genuine. She was definitely doing what she was passionate about. She looked over the selections before choosing a light blue sundress with multicolored abstract flower designs spattered across the material. "This one first. I *love* this."

Eva wanted to disagree, but she needed information

from Mrs. Tremant. She needed to earn her trust so she could worm her way into some answers. Playing dress-up, she suspected, was the most direct way to whatever remained of Tiffany's heart.

JOSHUA BIT HIS TONGUE, NOT WANTING TO POINT OUT that Eva was late as the door slammed behind her. She could have called. She'd known he would be cooking dinner. She could have texted. But he wasn't going to start a fight about it. That was pointless. He already knew how that fight would go. He'd say she should have called. She'd say she didn't answer to him. He'd say it was a matter of respect. She'd say if he wanted her respect, he'd better start showing her some.

So, no, he wasn't going to even start.

Instead, he took a slow pull from his beer to curb the words trying to push out of his mouth. Her shoes clicked on the floor as she crossed the room. He considered that for a moment. Her shoes clicked? Eva wore soft-soled shoes that wouldn't be heard when sneaking up on a perp —*suspect*. Her shoes didn't click.

She stopped at the end table, and he nearly choked on the drink sliding down his throat. If not for her piercing eyes and the hands-on-her-tiny-hips posture, he might not have recognized her. Her light red hair had been highlighted with streaks of gold, and her outfit was...*not* Eva.

"Laugh, and I'll box your ears so hard they'll never stop ringing," she warned.

Yeah. That was definitely Eva.

"I'm not laughing," he said as he stared at the long slit in her sundress. The pale skin of her thigh poked through the parted pink material. Her long hair had a newer, more fashionable cut. Layers, or so he thought they were called, angled in toward her long neck, reminding him how soft the skin there was against his lips.

The heels on her feet all but begged him to release the straps and ease them off so he could massage her arches and earn one of those little moans of appreciation he loved so much. When they were dating, his favorite way to unwind after a long day was to sink into her oversize tub, him on one end, her on the other, and talk about their days as he washed her legs and feet.

He wouldn't say he had a foot fetish by any means, but seeing her in those heels made him wonder if he should develop one.

"You're staring," Eva pointed out.

"Can't. Stop." His answer was honest. He lowered the beer to his lap to hide the evidence of his out-of-control body and grazed over her leg again. "What are you wearing?"

Dropping onto the sofa, Eva exhaled her frustration. The material parted, showing more of her leg than the designer had likely intended, but the dress likely wasn't intended for tomboys who never seemed to remember to sit "like a lady." Leaning to one side, she tugged the material and closed the two sides until her thigh was covered. "I was with Tiffany Tremant. She shops. *A lot.* Apparently I need more color in my wardrobe. I feel like a fucking paper doll. Remember those ones with the dresses and tabs... Oh, you probably got to play with trucks and roll around in the mud as a kid."

"I dissected my first maggot when I was six."

"You're such a nerd," she said, but her tone wasn't judgmental. She wasn't being mean. Her voice teased him as she grinned.

"I just meant... I didn't have trucks. I used Mom's steak knives to cut up bugs."

She lifted her top lip in a sneer. "Gross. I hope she knew so she could wash them really well."

"She bought me a set of scalpels when she found out."

Giggling, she shook her head. "You're lucky you still have fingers."

"Did she say anything useful? Tiffany, I mean."

Eva held up her hand in a silent bid for him to stop speaking. Pushing herself up, she walked into the bedroom. He didn't have to ask. She was in there scanning the room with her thermal camera. She came out a minute later, still in that dress, moving the camera around the room, checking for any sign of heat signatures that didn't belong. Then she followed the same movements with her infrared camera. She scanned the room and then finally sat back down.

Taking the beer from his hand, she rested her feet, still encased in those damn shoes, against the edge of the table.

He would have reminded her the table was tempered glass, but he was distracted by the way the material fell from her ankles and shins. Her long toes, with the nails now painted red, poked out from the tips, taunting him, begging him to kiss them like he used to. Okay. Maybe he did have a foot fetish. But only for Eva's cute little feet. He couldn't recall ever even noticing anyone else's.

"She isn't happy in her marriage," Eva stated, drawing his attention from her toes, "and I suspect she's having an affair, but she'd never admit either since it would imply that her perfectly molded life isn't so perfect. She did confirm that Shane Tremant and Neal Price are like peanut butter and jelly. Or like the James brothers," she added thoughtfully, comparing the HOA president and his friend to outlaws. "I'm not sure which one is Frank and which one is Jesse, though." She took a swig from his beer. "Actually, Shane is Jesse. Price doesn't have the charisma to be compared to Jesse James. He's a follower."

"Hmm. So they're robbing people?"

"I'm not sure what their crimes are yet, but they are definitely conspiring about something. They both set me on edge from the start." She took another drink, and Josh could practically see her mind spinning, laying out all the puzzle pieces to see how they fit. She was brilliant. And beautiful. And...sexy as hell.

He stroked a strand of newly dyed hair from her face, not comprehending that it was inappropriate until her eyes darted toward him. She always wore makeup, but it was different now. Usually the lines around her eyes were hard and distinct, but now they were blended and subtle. Apparently part of her makeover was adding longer lashes, a hint of sparkly eyeshadow, and somehow making all the layers of color appear as if she naturally looked like a fairy tale creature.

Swallowing hard, he dropped his hand. "I like this," he said as a way to justify his touch. "Looks nice."

"Thanks," she said quietly. She nearly jumped to her feet, swayed a bit on the high heels, and then got her balance. "Did you eat?"

"There are leftover chicken enchiladas in the fridge."

Her rigid posture relaxed a bit. "You're the best, Joshie. Tiffany dragged me to this horrible place that only sold salads. I'm starving. I'm going to change first."

He didn't respond to the nickname she used. That was clearly her way of irritating him to redirect his train of thought, which she would've had to be blind to miss. "Bring me a fresh beer when you come back," he called.

He stared at the television without actually seeing the documentary while he recalled every inch of her body in that dress. She didn't have the shape of a bodybuilder, but her muscles were firm, and the short sleeves and long slit showed off how toned she was. The heels accentuated her calves in a way that made him long to stroke his fingers over them once again. Not that he needed much prompting for that.

Refocusing on the television when the sounds of her in the kitchen drew him from his wayward thoughts, he tried to remember what he'd been watching before she'd come home.

"Want me to heat up some for you?" she called.

He didn't. He'd eaten plenty by himself. "Sure," he called anyway, not wanting her to eat alone—even if she deserved to for being late.

Jumping up, he joined her in the kitchen. While she scooped enchiladas, he opened two beers. Then he leaned back and watched her stretch to reach the microwave stowed way above the stove. She wore yoga pants now, but they clung to her in a way that was just as appealing as the long dress she'd changed out of.

"You know what I don't get?" she asked.

"Hmm?"

Leaning against the counter across from him, she gnawed at her lip. "At the potluck, Courtney and Melly were commenting on how close Shane Tremant and Neal Price are. Usually, friends that tight means that their families are tight, too. I spent about four hours with Tiffany today, and she didn't mention Brenda Price once. Not once. She ran through a list of people she wants to introduce me to, but the wife of her husband's so-called best friend didn't come up at all." She tapped her chin. "There's a story there. I swear, the more time I spend here, the more I realize this building is like an episode of freaking *Melrose Place*. Remember that show?"

"Vaguely."

"It was when primetime soap operas were a big thing. If two people weren't sleeping together, they were blackmailing each other. This place really seems like that. Doesn't it?"

"Actually, yes, it does."

She opened the microwave when it beeped and extracted a pile of steaming-hot enchiladas. "What are you watching?"

Shit. He'd tried to focus on the show, but it hadn't stuck. First he'd been frustrated at her lack of checking in, and then he'd been distracted by that damn dress. "Uh." He laughed softly. "Nothing interesting. We can change it."

She turned, plate in hand. "I thought we could start binging a new documentary."

Josh had already seen pretty much every documentary on his streaming service, but he nodded. He'd rewatch them all a dozen times if it meant she'd sit next to him. "Sounds good."

6

Eva forced a bright smile to her face as she held up a dish of berry cobbler when Courtney opened her door. Normally she would have found a million excuses to turn down a dinner invitation, but this was the perfect way to get inside another condo in the building.

Courtney's eyes widened as she accepted the dish. "Did you make this?" she asked Josh.

He actually blushed as he lifted his shoulders nonchalantly. "Yeah. Eva said you liked the dessert at the potluck."

"Liked is an understatement." She closed the door behind them, and Eva scanned the space. The layout was just like that of the unit she shared with Josh. A large living area with floor-to-ceiling windows to the left, an open kitchen to the right, and the only doors in the loft-like space were at the back—one to the half bath and one to the only bedroom.

Courtney had managed to soften the contemporary structure with large paintings of landscapes and cream-colored walls instead of the steel gray that Eva and Josh were living with. But the biggest difference? Courtney had a lot of knickknacks. Perfect for hiding cameras.

Eva cast her eyes toward Josh. He was still too flattered to catch on to Eva's plight. She really needed to scan this area for evidence. How as she supposed to do that discreetly when there were a million perfect hiding places?

She'd already told him the deal. She'd excuse herself to use the restroom, he'd distract Courtney, and Eva would slip into the bedroom to do a quick swipe with the thermal camera she'd tucked inside her purse. Then he'd distract their hostess again, and Eva would do the same in the living area. Only there would be no quick scan. The condo had more items on display than a museum. She'd need an hour to thoroughly search this room.

Shit.

Following Courtney and Josh to the kitchen, she ignored the chatter as she mentally calculated where a pervert would likely place a camera here. She'd have to make quick work of the areas she found most likely—if she even got the chance. The smoke alarm was the first choice, obviously, since that was where Wendi Carter had found the one in her condo. Eva took note of the location of the alarm, and then, slowly turning, selected the next item she'd check—a painting on the wall next to the bedroom door. The entire living area would be visible from that vantage point. High on a shelf, a cluster of framed photos caught her attention. A camera could be tucked onto a frame that high up and not be easily seen with the naked eye. Damn it. There were too many places for her to check in one visit.

"Earth to Eva," Courtney sang.

Eva spun, forcing that stupid perky smile to her face that she was getting too good at, as far as she was concerned. "Sorry," she gushed. "I'm just so taken with what you've done here. Your place is *adorable*."

Courtney pushed a glass of wine toward Eva. Clearly she'd offered the drink more than once while Eva had been focused on her search. "I love the location of this building. I don't love the design. I know contemporary is what most people here like, but all those shades of gray just felt so cold to me. I would love a little house in the country, but I wouldn't love the commute. When Neal Price selected my application, I couldn't pass it up, but I also couldn't live with the color scheme. Have you been to Melly's place yet?"

Eva didn't exactly hear the last part. Courtney's previous statement hung in her mind. "Neal selected your application?"

She nodded. "Of course. Condos in this area are really hard to come by. There must have been twenty applicants for this place." She tilted her head, and her ponytail full of blond curls fell over her shoulder. "Didn't he select you guys? My understanding is the HOA president selects everyone."

"Uh, we were on a waiting list," Josh offered and then lifted his brows at Eva.

She blinked a few times, trying to get her head back in the moment instead of examining the puzzle piece that had just fallen at her feet. Neal Price, HOA president and potential cohort of resident pervert Shane Tremant, was in charge of selecting who resided at Jupiter Heights? That seemed like a really important bit of information, and she was still processing it.

Josh slid his arm around her shoulders. "This is our first place together. Isn't it, babe?"

"Yeah."

"That's a big step," Courtney said lightly, but her face betrayed her lack of excitement for them. She seemed upset for some reason. She'd had that same disenchantment in her eyes when commenting on how lucky Eva and Melly were to have boyfriends. There was a story there.

Eva added that to the growing list of Jupiter Heights curiosities.

"Dinner smells great," Josh said.

The usual cheer returned to Courtney's eyes. "Thanks. I've never tried this recipe before, but I felt like I needed to go the extra mile since you are obviously a wonderful chef."

Josh's cheeks took on an even deeper shade of red as his shoulders did that goofy shrug thing again. Was he... flirting? In front of Eva? Okay. So they weren't *actually* a couple, but they were supposed to be, and his flirting with someone else, especially right in front of her, was completely unacceptable.

A tight coil of anger heated low in her stomach as she cast him a side glance, a silent warning that she was on to him. He didn't notice; he'd started nervous-rambling about chicken scaloppine and lemon glaze. Then he told Courtney he'd have to make dinner for her one night. Not just any dinner...penne with his special sauce. But only if she liked spicy food; if she didn't, he'd make something else.

Eva's stomach clenched. Had he *seriously* just offered to make his arrabbiata sauce with ground sausage for Courtney?

A spear of fury pierced Eva's heart. He made that for her. That was *her* favorite dish. The idea of him making sauce for Courtney made Eva want to put the bitch in a headlock and obliterate her perfectly painted face.

Courtney finally stopped grinning like a schoolgirl at Josh and winced a bit when she glanced Eva. Oh. Right. Josh had warned her about her lack of poker face. She imagined her jealousy was playing like a movie across her face for Courtney to witness.

No. Not jealousy. Jealousy wasn't the right word. Amazement. She was amazed that this twit had the audacity to bat her eyelashes and smile at Josh while he had his arm around his "girlfriend." What kind of skank ho—

Josh literally pulled Eva from her thoughts with a firm jerk that might have looked like a hug to someone else, but she knew a silent warning when she got one. If only Josh had the same ability to read her unspoken cautions, she wouldn't have had to give Courtney a death glare.

Peeling her lips back into a smile, Eva batted her eyes at the woman blatantly coming on to her man. "May I use your restroom?"

"Uh. Yeah," Courtney stuttered out. "Of course."

Spinning on her heels, she set her wineglass down on her way to the restroom. As soon as she was alone, she scoffed with disbelief. "Wow. What a bitch." She scanned for any obvious signs of a hidden camera as she dug her thermal camera from her bag. Muttering, still not quite believing the audacity Courtney had exhibited, she stared at the tiny screen and moved the camera face around, not finding anything unusual. Easing the door open, she listened to the muted conversation between Josh and Courtney, gritting her teeth when Courtney giggled. They were in the kitchen, out of view, as Eva and Josh had planned, but for some reason she no longer liked the idea of Josh distracting Courtney while Eva checked her condo.

Slipping into the bedroom, she stepped out of the doorway and behind the wall in case Courtney glanced toward the only two doors in her condo. Eva's gaze immediately fell to the queen-size bed, and her heart seized with an inexplicable ache. The antiqued white frame held layers of frilly pillows and intricately placed teddy bears. The scene was pure innocence.

For a moment, she pictured Josh there...with Courtney. He deserved the type of sweet woman who would decorate in lace and teddy bears. A nice woman. An innocent woman. One who looked at him with the kind of awe and enchantment Courtney had from the moment they'd walked into her condo.

Her pondering ended with a harsh slap of reality when Eva noticed handcuffs dangling from the headboard. *Oh.* Well, that changed things. A lot. This woman was no innocent. The pastels and prim façade were just that, and somehow things suddenly made sense. This picture of virtue set the scene for men who should be too old to be turned on by such things. The batting eyes were a bait and switch that Eva knew was often too tempting for the male half of the species to ignore.

What was that saying? Treat her like a queen during the day and a whore at night?

Someone had taken that to heart.

Aiming the heat reader, Eva pushed away the latest images of Josh that entered her mind...handcuffs included...and started searching for signs that the House of Kink was being watched. The sultry male laugh that drifted into the bedroom made Eva grind her teeth again. While the cat was away, huh?

Not that she was his cat. And he certainly wasn't her mouse. She had no reason to be jealous.

Damn it. There was that word again.

Scanning the room, Eva kept her ears open for any sign that Courtney was headed her way. She checked the clock, the lamp, the bookshelf, the display of dolls on the chest of drawers... Nothing. There was no sign of a camera in the bedroom. That left the living room and kitchen.

She groaned under her breath before rejoining Josh and Courtney in the kitchen. Courtney had the good sense to be standing a few feet from Josh when Eva returned. She slid up to his side and had her arm around his waist before she'd even comprehended her possessive action. His arm rested around her shoulder and hugged her to him with a smooth, gentle motion instead of the jerk he'd used before.

"Eva's better at grilling," he said, continuing whatever conversation they'd been having. "Much better, actually."

Courtney looked at her, as if suddenly reminded she and Josh weren't alone. "Oh, you'll have to teach me a thing or two sometime."

"Gladly." She hadn't meant to have a clip to her tone, but Courtney's smile froze.

This case should wrap up quickly—perhaps tonight, if she found a camera inside Courtney's condo—and then she and Josh would stop pretending to be more than they were. Until then, Courtney needed to consider Josh taken. Eva pressed even closer to him and grabbed her wine, taking a drink larger than was socially acceptable in an attempt to temper her frustration. This wasn't high school. She shouldn't have to lay claim to her man. Grown women should respect each other's relationships, not prey on them.

Looking at Courtney now, Eva didn't see a lonely

gossiper. She saw a troublemaker who couldn't resist the challenge of tempting a taken man.

"You okay?" Josh whispered in Eva's ear.

"Fine."

"You're tense." As if to prove his point, he put his hand to her shoulder and pressed his thumb into the muscle. His touch clearly wasn't intended in a romantic way, but she felt the pressure all the way to her crotch. He used to massage her all the time. Her shoulders, her back, her legs. Every inch of her. He once told her that rubbing his hands over her helped him put the things he'd seen during the day from his mind.

She couldn't imagine doing his job. Looking at corpses all day. Cutting them open. Yuck. No wonder he needed to focus on her warm, *live* body to clear his head. She didn't begrudge him that need. Especially since she usually benefited from it. His massages were incredible. She missed them. Not just his fingers kneading the knots in her back, but the way his touch soothed the tension that was like a live wire in her mind. She never seemed to be able to slow her thoughts, to stop trying to solve cases, until he'd pull her into a hot bath or one of their beds and start working his magic on her.

Eva inhaled as much garlic-scented oxygen as possible and let it out as she counted to five and then did it again. As always, the warmth and light pressure of his hand soothed the edge of her frustration and helped her breathe easier. She couldn't explain the feelings churning in her any more than she could deny them. Her primal urges usually didn't awaken outside of the gym where she practiced Krav Maga, but the need to stake claim to Josh was strong and borderline undeniable.

If she pressed herself any closer to him, she'd practically be hanging off him. Generally she didn't care for PDA, but she wasn't usually forced into a position to defend what was hers.

Not that Josh was hers. Not really.

The mental reminder should have convinced her to put space between them. Instead she set her wineglass down and entwined her fingers at his hip, effectively pinning him against her side. And making it clear where he belonged.

Courtney didn't say a word, but her eyes lingered on where Eva's hands rested, and her jaw muscles clenched a few times before she forced a smile back to her face. The atmosphere had changed. The neighborly camaraderie had taken on an electric edge that had popped up out of nowhere like a summer storm. One wrong move, and lightning could strike, causing the tension to combust. And not just between Eva and Courtney. Eva was just as aware of Josh's thumb brushing over her shoulder as she was of Courtney's dithery mood.

Eva hadn't expected the unspoken battle for Josh's attention when she'd accepted the dinner invitation, and perhaps that had been Courtney's plan, but Eva was never unprepared to do battle. Josh, on the other hand, seemed freaking oblivious, as always.

"Can I do anything to help?" Josh asked, as if Eva and

Courtney weren't having the staring contest to end all staring contests.

Courtney batted her eyes but with a little less flirtation behind the act this time. The little bitch had been testing the waters. Eva had made it clear she wasn't keen on what Courtney had been up to, but Josh hadn't. Courtney would take that as an invitation to continue her absurd behavior without realizing Josh was too dense to understand what she was up to.

"Thanks, Joshua," Courtney practically purred. "You are so sweet."

Her velvety tone caused Eva's stomach to tighten. Mostly because she knew men responded to that sort of seduction, and Eva had never been able to master it. If Josh knew how to blush on cue, she might not have been so concerned, but the red on his cheeks told her *and* Courtney she'd once again succeeded in flattering him. "Maybe you could just top off our wineglasses."

"Sure thing." He left Eva's side and went into the small kitchen area with Courtney.

The pang hit Eva again. Joshua looked *right* standing next to her unexpected adversary. They made a cute couple, and when Courtney looked over her shoulder and giggled, Josh's smile widened, as did the hole in Eva's chest.

Had they ever looked that good together? Had they ever had such easy rapport? Maybe early on, but things hadn't gone that smooth for long. Only a few months into dating, Josh had started questioning her. She'd started resenting him. And the whole thing had gone to hell.

Where had Courtney said she worked? Managing a bank. That was safe enough, wasn't it? Even if something did happen, there was security to protect her. Not like Eva. Eva *was* the security, and he couldn't handle that.

Josh handed Eva a refilled glass and met her at the edge of the counter before guiding her to the table set with three plates, each on their own side of the square table.

Conveniently.

Courtney managed to get her butt in the chair between Eva and Josh before either of them could make a move to sit next to the other. "I really hope you like this," she said, serving Josh first.

"It smells delicious," he offered.

Eva rolled her eyes at the chicken on her plate because nobody else would have noticed. Josh was too busy listening as Courtney broke down every step of creating the dish. Eva cut into the breast and snapped her teeth on the bite. Damn it. Her mouth actually started watering over the tenderness and perfect seasoning.

God, she hated this woman who was so much more deserving of the smile on Josh's face. And screw her for making perfectly crisp fresh green beans. And screw her twice for being so damned interested in his job and finding everything he said *so* funny.

Dinner seemed to drag on for hours. Eva did her best to keep her cool, but by the time Courtney cleared the table, she was fuming again. She had counted over forty ways to kill Courtney without even standing up.

"Eva," Josh said under his breath as he reached across the table.

She stared at his hand, wanting to use it to smack his forehead and give him a damn clue, but instead she put her palm to his and let him wrap his fingers around her hand as he looked at her with clear concern.

"What's going on?" he asked. "Did you find something in her room?"

She had to swallow the laugh that wanted to erupt from her. She'd found something all right. But Courtney's sexual interests were her business, not Eva's. Or Joshua's. Definitely *not* Joshua's. "No."

"Then what has you so worked up?"

Swallowing hard, she tried to ease the sharp edge in her tone. "Nothing."

He lifted a bushy brow over the rim of his glasses. "I'm throwing down the bullshit flag on that one. I'm not so great at reading body language, but even I can tell you're getting angrier by the moment."

"Am not."

"What's bothering you?"

"Nothing," she insisted.

"Liar."

Inhaling slowly, she narrowed her eyes. "Good dinner, Joshie?"

He stared at her for a long moment before grinning. "Not as good as anything you would make."

She practically snorted. She might...*might*...have believed that if he hadn't just spent the last twenty minutes gushing. Or if she hadn't sampled the damned delicious food herself.

"Do I still need to distract her so you can search the living room?"

"Yes."

Sitting back, he pulled his hand from hers. "I'm on it."

"Josh—"

She was going to ask his plan, but Courtney set down three dishes and then pulled her chair out, sliding it closer to Josh as she did.

Easing into her seat, she casually dropped her fingertips to his forearm. "This looks great, Joshua."

"Thank you, Courtney. I'm hoping you like it."

Her natural smile returned, and she flashed a triumphant glance at Eva. The temptation to drag her around by her hair returned. Digging in with her spoon, Courtney made a show of slowly pulling the utensil from between her lips and moaning as she rolled her eyes closed. "Amazing."

Jesus. Effing. Christ. Just jump him already, Eva seethed internally. She smiled across the table. "Wonderful as always, Josh."

"Thanks, Eva." He tipped his spoon in her direction. "This is Eva's favorite."

It wasn't, but she appreciated his attempt at reminding Courtney his "girlfriend" was in the room. Then he tipped his spoon too far and hit his wineglass, which spilled on his dessert...which splashed bright berry stains on his light blue dress shirt. "Oh, shoot!"

"Oh, don't worry." Courtney jumped to her feet and grabbed him by the hand. "I do that all the time. Come with me. We need to rinse your shirt before the stains set in."

And they were gone. Vanished in a flurry of pastels toward the bathroom. Eva had to admit she was impressed with Josh's creativity *and* with Courtney's boldness. If she hadn't wanted the room to herself, she would have jumped up just as quickly and intervened. No doubt Courtney was in there unbuttoning Josh's shirt this very second. He always wore an undershirt. Always. So...at least she wouldn't see the little patch of hair that traveled from his belly button into his waistband.

Closing her eyes, Eva huffed out a breath and forced her fists to relax. Turning her head, tuning in to the voices and giggles from the other room, she confirmed Courtney was taking control of the situation. She pushed herself up. She didn't have a moment to lose focusing on unimportant things. She pulled the thermal reader from her purse and started scanning the shelves of knick-knacks. Half-assed listening to Josh telling their hostess about other shirts he'd ruined, Eva continued the mission —the only reason she was still sitting there tolerating Courtney's behavior. The first set of shelves was clean, as was the second. The smoke detector had no suspicious signs, nor did the picture frames Eva expected to see glowing with a heat signature. But as she turned and scanned the table next to the front door, something white just slightly behind the front right leg of the table caught her eye.

A quick check on the events in the bathroom confirmed the water was still running as Courtney proved how domestic she was. Huffing, Eva marched to the table, bent at the waist, and clicked her tongue.

"Gotcha," she whispered. After pulling a latex glove from her bag, she used it to snatch the tiny device from where it'd been taped to the table leg and dropped it into an evidence bag. If she hadn't seen the signature, she never would have seen it, even if she'd been looking. Whoever had hid it there was clever. Very clever.

But not nearly as clever as Eva.

Josh stepped back when Courtney put her hand to his arm. Again. He wanted to leave the small confines of the bathroom before he had to pry her off him. He'd never seen someone so aggressive. And that said a lot, considering whom he hung out with. Eva and the HEARTS were far from subtle, but even Eva hadn't jumped on him until they'd reached a certain point in their relationship.

Once she knew he was just as interested, she'd pounced. Literally. She'd asked if he wanted her to kiss him, he'd said yes, and she was on him. Her mouth pressed to his, and her body wrapped around him so tightly he hadn't been able to breathe. He would have gladly suffocated if she hadn't broken the kiss first.

But this woman? Coming on to him like this? In front of his girlfriend? Okay, his *supposed* girlfriend. This was the biggest turnoff he'd ever seen. Even if he had been interested in her before this dinner, he would have lost it the moment she started trying to take him away from Eva. And he had no doubt that was the game she was playing. He wasn't a stud like Shane Tremant, or even close, but he wasn't stupid, either. This woman was on the hunt, and she'd decided Josh was her prey. Despite Eva shooting daggers at her from across the table.

Stupid, stupid woman.

But he had to admit that seeing Eva act jealous was a treat he never thought he'd see. She kept her cool. Always. But something about Courtney's behavior had really set her off in a way he hadn't anticipated. He was quite certain if it weren't for her camera hunt, she would have punched Courtney's lights out and dragged Joshua from the condo, whether he wanted to leave or not.

He would have left. In fact, he would have scooped Eva up like he'd used to do and carried her all the way back to their bedroom. He was tempted to do that anyway. If he thought she'd allow it, he would.

"I think that's it," Courtney said, holding his shirt up to the light. "I think I got them all out."

"Hey, that's great. Thanks so much."

She balled his shirt up and twisted the material to squeeze out the water. "Oh, it's no problem at all." She looked over her shoulder and batted her eyelashes in a way that most men likely found appealing. "I'm happy to help. Are you sure you don't want me to wash your undershirt?" She nearly pouted. "Those stains will never come out."

He lifted his hands, showing he didn't have a care in the world. "Nobody but Eva sees my undershirts." Zing. Feel that point hit home.

She didn't. She just stuck her lip out a bit more as she turned to face him and heaved her breasts out. "I don't mind." She reached for the hem of the white T-shirt, but he caught her wrist.

"Neither does Eva. She's the only one I need to impress."

That seemed to finally get through to her. Her smile faltered, and the arch in her back returned to normal so her breasts weren't popping out. "She doesn't seem to like me. Which is odd. We had such a nice conversation the other day."

Reaching around her, careful to leave plenty of space, he grabbed his shirt. "She had a long day at work."

"At the library?"

He tightened his jaw at Courtney's mocking tone. "*Yes*. At the library."

"How cute." Her batting eyes suddenly didn't seem nearly as charming. Not that he'd been charmed. But he hadn't seen them as menacing, like he did now. Something about this woman was off. Her mask had slipped a bit in that moment, and he caught a glimpse of a darkness that was unsettling.

His sense of protectiveness flared. He wanted to close the distance between them, not to accept what Courtney had been subtly offering since he'd stepped foot in her apartment but to warn her off whatever game she was playing. The fact that she had an ulterior motive to her flirtations was suddenly clear. What that motive was wasn't. But his nerves were instantly on high alert, and he was tempted to call her on what he'd seen.

Eva had taught him better, though. *Keep cool, Joshua.* He heard her voice run through his mind.

He leaned against the doorframe, ignoring the drips from his bundled shirt. Courtney, however, glanced down at the sound of the rhythmic *splat-splat-splat*, and her smile faded.

"Just to be clear," he said in a tone that wasn't nearly as laid-back as it had been for the rest of the evening, "Eva's the only woman for me. Ever. In any capacity."

Her eyes iced over for a moment before she smiled. "I didn't imply otherwise."

"Doing so would be pointless."

She made a move like she was starting for the door, so he put his hand to the jamb, wet shirt and all. Her cheeks flushed as she watched what he suspected to be streams of water running to the floor. He didn't know how much more time Eva needed, but if she didn't wrap things up soon, she was going to get busted. Short of taking Courtney up on her offers—which he'd already made clear wasn't an option—he was running out of ways to keep her occupied.

The smile that curved Courtney's lips sent a chill down Joshua's spine. She was almost pleased with his statement. She tugged at the hemline of his stained undershirt and took a step closer to him.

"I do love a challenge."

"This isn't a game, Courtney."

Leaning in so close he could feel her breath, she whispered, "Everything is a game, *Joshua*."

So caught off guard by her movement and hushed words, he let her slip by him. Shit. He stepped out of the bathroom after her. The minx was rushing toward where Eva was clearing off the table.

"Oh, don't do that," Courtney insisted. "You're my guest."

Eva put her hand on her hip and tilted her head. "Oh, but you were so busy taking care of Josh, I just had to do something." Her tone was patronizing and her eyes thin slits.

"I don't mind at all." She set the stack of dishes on the sink and looked at Josh again, her flirtation renewed. "I had so much fun talking with you. You are so interesting. Isn't he?" She looked at Eva.

Josh draped his arm over Eva's shoulder and ran his fingertips over her upper arm as he hugged her to his side. Pressing his lips to her head, he stared at Courtney, making sure she knew the point he was making. "Eva and I can spend hours talking about nothing. Even uninteresting things. That's the best part about being in a relationship. Don't you think, babe?"

Playing her part, Eva snuggled a bit closer to him. "Definitely one of the better parts, but I can think of one or two things that top the list."

He chuckled, kissed her head again, and then gently pushed her toward the door. "Thanks for dinner, Courtney. I think we should head out. Eva's had a long day."

"At the library," Courtney pointed out.

Eva tensed under his arm. "That Dewey Decimal system is a real bitch sometimes."

"I bet."

Josh nudged Eva again, and they headed right for the door, not giving Courtney an opportunity to intervene. The door closed behind Josh, and he lifted his brows in warning. "Bite your tongue for two more minutes."

She exhaled a long breath but did as he said. However, the moment they stepped inside the elevator, she turned on him. "What the fuck was that?"

He held his hands up. "Don't blame me."

"I'm not." Her tone wasn't any less bitter, though. "Who the hell acts like that? I have never seen—" She stopped when the elevator door slid open and they walked to their door, but the moment they were inside, she threw her purse on the sofa and spun, hands on hips. "She was practically sitting on your dick by the time dinner was over."

"Uh, let's not put it that way."

She glared at him. "What happened in the bathroom? Did she touch you?"

"No."

"I'll break her fucking arm if she touched you."

He lifted his hands again. "The only thing that happened was that I made it perfectly clear to her that I was not interested in any woman but you."

Eva stared at him, obviously gauging his response. "That's what you said?"

"Yes. That's *exactly* what I said." Closing the distance between them, he brushed her hair from her face. "Do you really think I'd want the kind of woman who hits on a man right in front of his girlfriend?"

"You'd be surprised how many men find that irresistible."

"I'm not one of them." He saw the doubt playing in her eyes, and he didn't blame her. That was quite a show Courtney had put on. "You know me well enough to know that."

"I do," she said with soft affection. "You're a good guy, Josh."

For some reason, saying that seemed to hurt her, but before he could push, she pulled away from him.

"I found a camera."

Shit. He'd actually forgotten that was what this entire evening had been about. "Where?"

"Underneath the table by the door." She pulled an evidence bag out of her purse and showed it to him. "First image should be of whoever put it there."

"Aren't you going to tell Courtney?"

She stared at him.

"There was a camera in her home."

"I know that. I'll tell Neal."

"Neal? Eva, he—"

"Is the president of the HOA and my client."

"And, as you've pointed out before, a possible suspect."

She gnawed at her lip. "Good point. I'm not telling him either."

"But Courtney—"

"May blow the entire case if I tell her who I am and what I found. I need to find out who is planting these cameras first. I will keep an eye on her. Nothing will happen to her. Unless she pisses me off again." She pulled a little black case out of her purse as she moved toward her laptop. She pushed a button to bring the machine to life, tapped in her username and password, and then opened the black case and pulled out tools he suspected were used to pry open locks.

"Eva—"

"Don't, Josh. I don't break laws."

"Carrying a set of lockpicks implies otherwise."

She looked up at him. "One of the things people hire me to do is try to break into their business to test their security. I only break into places that want me to. Okay? Now stop distracting me. I want to see what's on this card, but I have to get it out without compromising any prints. I need to focus."

He snapped his lips closed as she pried the little device open and then used tweezers to pull the SD card out of the camera. Sitting closer than necessary out of his need to connect, he changed the subject. "Listen, something is off about that woman."

Eva snorted. "You're telling me."

"No, Eva. When I told her I wasn't interested, she was angry. She didn't say it, she didn't show it, but her eyes..."

She leaned back a bit as she turned her face to him. Probably because he was too close for her to get a good look at him. "What do you mean?"

"I can't explain it. I just got a sense that she wasn't used to getting rejected and she didn't like it. At all."

"I'm sure she's not used to it. You saw her. She's...perfect."

"No. She's good at faking perfect. But something is going on there."

Eva returned her focus to putting the card in her laptop to view the contents. "I want you to steer clear of her." She glanced back. "Not because she wants to jump your bones but because I believe you. That there's something wrong with her. No sane person acts that way. She doesn't even know us. It was like she was..." She leaned back a bit.

"What?"

Eva smirked. "Uh. Her bedroom was...not what I was expecting."

He lifted his brows. "Oh, come on, Eva. You can't leave it at that."

"I don't want to violate her privacy."

"Seriously? She would have let me have sex with her in the bathroom if I'd asked, and you don't want to violate *her* privacy?" His arrow hit the mark. Her eyes hardened and her determination to respect Courtney vanished.

"Everything was satin and lace until I took a closer look and noticed handcuffs on the headboard. She isn't sweet and innocent at all. Not that there's anything wrong with bondage." She glanced at him, and he'd be damned if her cheeks didn't turn three shades darker. "If you're into that. But add that with her less-than-subtle flirting, and... I'm not sure she wasn't testing my willingness to share as much as she was testing your willingness to be shared."

He creased his brow. "What?"

"She's got some kink going on, Joshie. She was checking to see if we do, too."

"That was...bold."

She nodded as the program finished loading. "Some people are."

"That doesn't explain her getting angry when I said I wasn't interested."

"No, and I still want you to stay away. She is far too determined to sink her nails into you." She smirked. "Literally, I'd guess."

He shook his head as if the idea disgusted him. The only part of the idea he didn't like was it being Courtney's nails instead of Eva's. "There," he said, nodding toward the screen.

The camera images came to life. The darkness of a hand pulled away and revealed the country décor that had softened Courtney's condo. What it didn't reveal was the person who had placed the camera. All the screen showed from the vantage point under the table were dark pants that could have belonged to anyone.

"Snoop around," Eva encouraged under her breath. "You're already in there. Snoop around."

He didn't. He'd placed the camera, and that was that.

"Damn it," Eva cursed. She pushed the button to increase the speed of the replay.

Josh swallowed. "What are you doing? We can't watch this. This is a violation...a real violation...of Courtney's privacy."

"I'm not looking to see what Miss Hot Pants is up to. I just want to see if the owner of this camera pokes his head down to check on it."

They sat in silence for what seemed an eternity as Courtney went about her day in high speed. About two hours into real time on the video, Courtney went to the door and let someone in. Another woman's legs appeared on the screen, but they were too close to the table to see more than Courtney's long skirt and a white dress falling just to someone's knees.

Josh widened his eyes as the legs got closer together. Very close together. "I think they must be hugging."

"Or something else," Eva offered when the white skirt moved up a few inches.

The women greeted each other—intimately, apparently—before walking deeper into the apartment. They disappeared into the bedroom.

"Yup. Definitely something else." She grinned as she

gently bumped against Josh. "Hey, maybe she wasn't trying to get into *your* pants after all."

"She was flirting with *me*."

Laughing, she patted his knee several times before speeding up the replay again.

He glanced at the time marker on the screen. Almost an hour had gone by. "They've been in there a long time."

"Women have more stamina than men."

"Most men lose an erection after ejaculating because—"

"I don't care about the science, Joshie. Just pointing out that when both partners can have multiple orgasms, the show runs a bit longer."

He shifted as images that shouldn't be rolling through his mind rolled through his mind. Several times. Eva had said that bit about multiple orgasms with too much authority. Like she'd tested out the theory. And that made his mind go places it shouldn't.

"Are you picturing me having sex with a woman, Josh?"

"No." Damn. His voice had cracked. "Maybe."

She smirked. "Good. Oh, there they are." She turned the video to normal speed as Courtney and her lover left the bedroom. "Well. I'll be goddamned."

"Isn't that..."

"A thoroughly satisfied Tiffany Tremant." Leaning back, she chuckled. "Wow. I take it back. This is way better than *Melrose Place*."

7

Eva offered Wendi Carter a reassuring smile. The woman looked exhausted, as if she hadn't slept in weeks. Considering that the security of her home had been so blatantly violated, maybe she hadn't. Eva had been as patient as she could. The last time she'd called Wendi, she had piled on the guilt—she really needed to meet with Eva...before this happened to someone else.

Wendi sank onto her plush teal sofa. "Thanks for your patience. This has been a trying week for me. I should have gone to the police. I don't know why I let Neal talk me out of it."

"Can you tell me more about that? About why he didn't want you to go to the police?"

Sinking back onto a pile of decorative pillows in bright whites and yellows, she shrugged. "He said it would be bad for the community. He said everyone would be terrified and start turning on each other. I could see how that would happen," she said, lifting bloodshot eyes to Eva. "I can't stand to be here. I've been staying with my boyfriend. I'm only here long enough to get clothes."

"Well, thank you for giving me a chance to talk to you."

Wendi lifted her gaze, scanning the room with the kind of paranoia usually saved for conspiracy theorists. "I loved this place. Everything about it. I decided last night that I'm going to sell. I don't want to live here anymore."

Eva nodded. "I understand. Did you or Mr. Price look for additional cameras after finding the one in your smoke detector?"

A mirthless laugh left her. "I tore this place apart. I didn't find anything."

"Would you mind if I searched before we go any further?"

"No. Go ahead."

Opening her bag, Eva pulled out her thermal camera.

Wendi leaned forward, staring at it. "What's that?"

"Cameras, even small ones, radiate heat. This will show me a little white aura." She gave Wendi a kind smile. "You can get one online for pretty cheap."

Wendi didn't have to say she intended to buy one. A resolute light sparked in her eye, a bit of confidence that she had lacked before. She'd get one and probably spend the next six months or so scanning everything she saw, tearing small appliances apart before realizing she was seeing something other than a camera. Eventually she'd start to feel comfortable with her surroundings again, but

Eva knew from experience that victims of crimes like this never quite felt as secure as they had before they'd been violated.

"You know, there are a lot of ways to quickly scan for hidden cameras. Why don't we set up a time for you to come by my office, and I'll show you some things?"

"That'd be really great." A sheen of tears sprang to her eyes, and she hugged herself a little tighter. "I'm still a bit out of sorts."

"It will take a while, but that will get better." Focusing on the tiny screen, Eva walked around the room, talking to Wendi as she did, showing her the difference in the colorations on the screen. She was almost disappointed when she finished going over the condo and hadn't found a camera tucked away somewhere, but she wasn't surprised.

Whoever the culprit was, he'd know that the other camera had been found and would have collected any others he'd tucked around the area. Easing into the straight-backed chair across from Wendi's sofa, Eva returned to her questioning. "Have you had any run-ins with anyone here that left you uneasy?"

"Not run-ins exactly."

"But something did happen?"

She shrugged, as if trying to dismiss the notion.

Eva wasn't so quick to let it go. "You know how sometimes when you're walking alone at night and you get a feeling that you need to hurry, and you start rushing along but then laugh it off as soon as you're safe inside your car?

That happens because your brain has picked up something that it hasn't quite processed yet but recognizes as potential danger. It's called intuition, and it is a powerful thing that humans have had forever. It gives us that flight response before we even know we need it. If your intuition has told you something, no matter how small, I'd really like to know."

Eva sat patiently as Wendi stared at her hands.

"I never liked the way Shane Tremant looked at me. He's just so...open with his staring. Like he thinks every woman is on display just for him."

Shane Tremant. Not surprising. The comment also brought a natural turn to his wife and Eva's need to clarify if Wendi had ever slept with the woman. If two of Tiffany's lovers had a camera placed in their condos, that drew an even larger red arrow at Shane Tremant's head.

"And his wife? Did you ever have any contact with her?"

A bitter laugh ripped from Wendi. "She cornered me in the women's locker room a few weeks ago and told me if I didn't stop flirting with her husband, she'd file a harassment claim against me." She furrowed her brow as pink roses bloomed on her cheeks. "Everybody here knows what that man is like, but nobody will do anything because he is Neal's friend and Neal runs this place. And Tiffany... That bitch knows her husband is a snake. I swear she gets off on shaming his victims."

"Have you ever been friendly with Tiffany?"

"No. She's insane. I keep my distance from both of them."

Eva nodded her understanding. "Did you tell her it was Shane who was crossing the line?"

"Yeah, but she didn't believe me. She's not stupid. She knows what he's like. That's why I think she enjoys it. She enjoys the drama his behavior brings."

"Some people do. What about Neal Price? Have you had any issues with him?"

She frowned. "He's not as obvious as Shane, but I've caught him looking at me in ways that made my skin crawl." Rolling her eyes, she huffed out a breath. "I'm not trying to sound egotistical."

Giving her another reassuring smile, Eva said, "You are a beautiful woman, but that's not a requirement for men like that. They aren't interested in physical beauty as much as they are in the power they feel in knowing they make someone, women usually, feel inferior."

"And Tiffany? How do you explain her behavior?"

Not that she was disappointed that Wendi hadn't been sleeping with Tiffany, but it did take a bit of air from her sails to think the lead wasn't as strong as she'd suspected it to be just a few moments ago. "I think she's insecure. Scared. Addicted to drama. Any number of reasons." She changed directions. "I have to ask a question that you may feel uncomfortable answering, but I need the truth. I promise I won't share the information with anyone. Have you ever had sex with someone who lives in this building? Male or female? Anyone?"

"No. I was dating my boyfriend when I bought this place. We were talking about him moving in here until this happened."

"How well do you know Courtney Jamison?"

She shrugged. "Not well. Why?"

Instead of answering, Eva said, "Someone obviously broke in to place the camera. Do you know how he gained entry?"

"There was no damage to the door. They had to have had a key."

"Does the office have keys to condos? For maintenance or security purposes?"

"Not that I know of."

"Have you given anyone an extra key?"

She shook her head. "Other than my boyfriend, no. And no, he didn't do this."

Eva didn't pause before asking, "How can you be sure?"

"He was out of town the week it happened. He left on Sunday morning for Boston to attend a conference. The battery was in the smoke alarm on Sunday afternoon. On Thursday night, there was a camera. He didn't do it."

"When you go to the amenities here, the gym or the pool, where do you put your keys?"

"Each condo is assigned a locker."

"And you use it?"

"Yes. I've had money go missing before. Not here but another building I used to live in. I always use a locker now." Her eyes lit. "I lost my keys. About a month ago. At the last potluck. I set them on the table because my dress didn't have pockets. They were missing for about twenty minutes before Cody Price found them under a chair."

"Cody...Neal's daughter?"

"The girl who always looks like she's on her way to a funeral."

Eva snickered. She'd had the same assessment. Jotting notes, she confirmed in her mind that the voyeur was definitely someone within the community—not that she'd really suspected Wendi's boyfriend, but he did have access to her condo and possibly the others. The flashing arrows continued to point to Shane Tremant and possibly Neal Price.

"Why did you call Neal Price instead of the police?"

"That's the protocol. Unless it's a situation for 911, tenants are supposed to call the HOA president."

"Has it always been that way?"

She nodded. "Ever since I moved in."

Eva was confident she knew, but she asked anyway. "And who was the HOA president when you moved in?"

"Shane Tremant," she whispered, her eyes widened. "He did this, didn't he?"

"I don't know."

"That sick son of a bitch. I'll gouge his eyes out."

"Tempting as that may be, I don't recommend it. Messier than it sounds."

Wendi smiled, but the amusement on her face didn't last. "Neal knew, didn't he?"

"I don't know anything yet, Wendi. I have my suspicions, but I don't *know* for certain. I need you to stay away from them. I can't accuse either of them of anything until I know for certain, and if they think that I'm on to them, they could cover their tracks more than they have already. Can you do that for me?"

"Yeah."

Eva got up. "I'm sorry this happened to you."

Exhaling as she stood, Wendi nodded. "I feel like I'm being watched every minute of every day. I think I'll take you up on your offer to go by your office."

Digging a business card out of her pocket, Eva held it out to her. "Call me anytime. Even if you just want me to come sweep your condo for cameras. I don't mind."

Wendi nodded. "Thank you."

Eva left her to finish packing as she debated her next move.

Josh tried to use his fire breath, but sitting cross-legged on the padded gym floor seeking his Zen, he sounded more like an asthmatic lizard. "I still don't get this." He grunted when the back of Eva's hand collided with his diaphragm.

"Feel that?"

"Hard to miss you punching me."

"Did you feel how the air left the bottom of your lungs?"

"I felt you punching me."

She let out her fire breath—a guttural-sounding whoosh of air that was supposed to help her connect with her inner peace. "Push from deep down, Joshua. Don't use your lungs; use your abs."

"Shouldn't I be blowing smoke or something?" He pulled his lips into a sarcastic grin. "Fire breath."

She rolled her head to him, causing the messy bun on her head to plop to one side. "Breath of fire, Josh." Untangling her feet, she hopped up with the ease of a bouncing ball. Situating herself behind him, she grabbed his shoulders, rammed her knee into his spine, and forced his posture straight as a series of joints popped and released pressure he hadn't noticed before.

"Ow."

"Hush," she insisted. "Deep breath. Through your nose and hold it."

He pulled in as much oxygen as he could while she continued to torture him. He had to wonder how much of that had to do with her frustration that Rene had called to let her know that the camera she'd dropped off at HEARTS was clean. There wasn't a single fingerprint on the thing. She'd been so upset, she'd slammed her phone down hard enough that Josh had checked to make sure the screen hadn't cracked. Rene wasn't giving up. She was going to see if there was a way to trace who had bought the camera, but Eva had been angry all the same. She wanted this case wrapped up, and the fact that the camera hadn't shown the bad guy and he hadn't left trace evidence was making her angrier and angrier the more she thought about it.

"Eva," he grunted out after too many moments had passed. "Can I exhale now?"

"Oh, sorry. Tremant walked in. I was watching him check out my ass in the mirror."

Josh released his breath with a growl and opened his eyes, ready to take on the giant if necessary.

Eva pulled his shoulders back into position, popping even more vertebrae. "Close your eyes."

He continued scowling at the man adding weights to the straight bar.

"Your shoulders are getting tense."

"I hate him."

"You and every woman he's ever met. Now close your eyes."

Straightening his back in an attempt to get her knee out of his spine, he inhaled.

"Hold it," she instructed. "If he knows that his wife is sleeping with a woman, do you think he'd even care?"

"Doubt it," he grunted. "He's the type who would ask to participate."

She removed the pressure on his back and put her lips to his ear. "And you aren't? Exhale."

He did, too quickly thanks to the image that flashed through his mind at her whispered words. And when she told him to take another breath, he did. Then her hand slid around his chest and she pressed her palm to his stomach. The warmth of her skin against his thin shirt consumed him. She smelled of jasmine—sweet and a little spicy. Josh smiled, thinking how the scent so perfectly represented Eva. Sweet but spicy. Kind but tough. Gentle but hard. So full of contradictions she made his head spin.

Eva kept her voice quiet as she spoke. "I wonder if he put the cameras in not to catch them but to *watch* them. Maybe Tiffany knows."

"But there wasn't a camera in Courtney's bedroom. If Tiffany knew, wouldn't she have had sex with Courtney in view of the camera?"

"Good point. Hold your breath."

He refilled his lungs and held as she brushed her fingers over his shirt, over his muscles, lingering lightly. Damn. He missed how she'd used to caress him. But then she jabbed his solar plexus so hard, all the air rushed out of him in a desperate grunt. Standing up, she patted him on the head like a dog who'd learned to sit. "That was better."

"Jesus, Eva."

She leaned over his shoulder and whispered again, earning his forgiveness with her close proximity. "I'm going to keep him distracted. You *very* discreetly watch him. See if you catch him doing anything suspicious."

Josh wanted to protest. The idea of her intentionally drawing some pervert's attention made him uneasy, but he kept his mouth shut. This was her job. This was what she did. She knew what she was doing. She could take care of herself.

He replayed the new mantra he'd been telling himself over and over. *Let Eva do her job, Joshua.*

Still sitting, as if he were working on his meditative practice, he opened his eyes enough to watch Tremant's reflection in the mirror as Eva stood as tall as her short frame allowed, stretching her arms over her head and arching her back. The prick paused, smirked, and focused on the tight bralette barely containing Eva's breasts.

When she'd emerged from their bedroom in what Josh would consider underwear, he'd swallowed hard. She had looked down at the short shorts and told him they were the same type volleyball players wore. And the sports bra? Perfectly acceptable in a gym setting. Her pale skin shone like a silver pearl against the dark blue spandex of her outfit. He stood motionless, watching her muscles bulge and twist over bone as she pulled her hair into a messy bundle that reminded him how the strands got tangled around his fingers as he buried himself deep inside her.

The little hint of a mischievous grin on her face made him suspect she knew just how hot she looked. The suspicion was confirmed when she patted his chest as she headed for the door.

"I'm on the hunt for a voyeur, Josh. Old sweats and a ratty T-shirt isn't the right bait for this fishing expedition."

He'd kept his mouth shut. The idea of a pervert seeing nearly every part of her precious body didn't sit well with him, but...

Let Eva do her job, Joshua.

Grinding his teeth, feeling anything but in touch with his peaceful side, he watched through squinted eyes as Tremant licked his lips while Eva bent over at the waist to touch her toes. Josh couldn't see from his angle, but from the dramatic way the man bit his lip and leaned back, he imagined Eva's tiny shorts had pulled tight against her sex.

Exhaling slowly as he clenched his fists, he had to focus all his energy on staying put. He wanted to jump up and put himself between the man's prying eyes and Eva's skimpy shorts.

"Listen to you," she teased. "Getting in touch with your breath of fire."

"I want to kill him."

"Is he watching?"

Josh ground his teeth even closer together. "Intently."

"Just remember. If he's got his eyes on me, he's leaving innocent bystanders alone."

Another breath of fire left him. "I know how to remove eyeballs without causing damage to the surrounding tissue."

"Careful, Dr. Simmons. You know what that sexy office talk does to me."

Josh actually chuckled. Before he could stop himself, he ran his hand down Eva's leg. She tensed but didn't smack him away like he expected. He supposed she couldn't without making Tremant wonder why she wouldn't want her boyfriend touching her.

The temperature was cooler in the gym than in the rest of the building, but her skin was warm against his palm. Her calf muscles contracted as she twisted at the waist, still stretching in a way that gave the pervert a perfect view of her assets. Her cheeks had blushed, and that knowing smirk curved her lips.

"Whatcha doing, Joshie?" she whispered.

He gripped her leg. "Reassuring myself you could kick his ass if needed."

"I could kick his ass five times if needed." She winked before standing upright and stepping from his grasp.

Watching the mirror again, he narrowed his eyes when Tremant studied Eva's every move as she stepped onto a treadmill. Josh sighed, knowing from experience how those little shorts were going to start riding up her ass once she started jogging. She might as well be naked, and he had no choice but to stand back and watch Tremant watch her.

A growl left him, and he didn't even bother to hide it.

8

Eva spread paperwork and notes across the conference room table and settled in with a cup of coffee to review all the evidence she'd collected since moving into the condo. She still got the heebie-jeebies when she thought of how Tremant been looking at her during the potluck. Tiffany might have her husband on a pedestal, but the favor definitely wasn't returned. He'd barely noticed she wasn't at his side.

Something was off with that man. She tapped her fingers. Maybe he was just testing the waters with the key fob, just seeing how natural it felt to hold it the way he was. Maybe he was working up the courage to be so bold as to record his victims right to their faces.

Most voyeurs liked the thrill of watching without being caught. Holding the actual camera might heighten his perverse enjoyment. He might even be preparing to do a little upskirting on his unsuspecting neighbors. Now that every phone came with a camera, the act of snapping a photo or grabbing a few seconds of video under a woman's hemline had become more of an issue than it should be in a civilized society.

She wouldn't be surprised if he had been working up the courage to utilize his *key fob* at a social gathering. Hell. Maybe he already had.

She shuddered at the thought, recalling how many short skirts had been worn at the recent potluck. "Creep."

Alexa walked into the conference room and dropped into a chair across the table. "Have you nailed the voyeur yet?"

"Not yet. I have an idea but nothing concrete."

Alexa finished pulling her long, dark hair into a bun and wrapping the haphazard mess with an elastic band. "What does your gut tell you?"

"There is something very fishy about this guy." She tapped a picture of Shane Tremant.

"Your new BFF's hubby?"

Ignoring the jab—she'd taken more than enough of them since explaining in the morning meeting why she'd gone on a shopping spree and gotten a makeover on the agency's dime—she tapped the photo of Neal Price. "He's sleazy, too."

"Isn't that the guy who hired us?"

"Well, he couldn't very well ignore a tenant reporting a hidden camera in her condo, could he? But he didn't take it to the police, did he? He probably thinks he's smart enough to worm his way out of getting caught. He's the only one who knows about the investigation. He can pacify Wendi, keep an eye on me, and remove any cameras he may have previously hidden. And he conveniently *lost* the recovered camera, so we couldn't review it. That's a red flag and flashing neon sign all wrapped up in one."

"That is convenient." Alexa read over some of Eva's notes. "Has Sam found any of the footage online?"

"Not yet."

"She's checked the Dark Web, too?"

"She's monitoring, but nothing is going easy in this case. The camera was found. And then lost. There are security cameras, but the company doesn't retain footage for more than an hour or so. Someone is recording but not posting the footage anywhere online that we can find. Granted, we can't search all those private for-sale sites, but certainly something would have leaded by now and Sam would have found it." She shook her head. "The usual crumbs are missing, and it's setting me on edge. I'm overlooking some major clues, and I don't like it."

Alexa's lips curved into a supportive smile. "You'll get it, Eva. We're all here to help if you need to bounce things around. So. How's Josh handling this?" She lifted her light brown eyes and batted her lashes as if she were as innocent as a cherub.

Aha! The real reason her co-worker had come to check on her. The women of HEARTS were more like sisters than teammates, so Eva wasn't the slightest bit surprised that one of them would sneak in to get intel on

Joshua. She knew what Alexa was really asking, and it had nothing to do with how Joshua was *handling* his first undercover assignment. But she wasn't going to answer the real question. She wasn't going to tell anyone, not even herself, how nice it was to come home to Josh every night.

She'd missed the companionship. Not Josh. She'd missed having company. But she couldn't say that without Alexa trying to pick her intentions apart and turn her words into more than they were. So no. She wasn't going to say that. Instead, she said, "He seems to be doing okay. I told Holly having him there was pointless. He's more of a risk than an asset."

"How so?"

"Holly's worried about what could happen if I catch someone in the condo. She wants Josh there for backup. But what if Josh walks in on someone? He is completely incapable of protecting himself. And if he's there, I'm going to be distracted trying to keep him out of harm's way." Lifting her hands, palms up, point made, she said, "More risk than an asset."

"Well, you were right. We couldn't put one of us there with you, and Holly felt it was too dangerous to be there on your own. Josh was the logical answer."

Eva snorted, recalling how they'd laughed just that morning as she'd had to balance him so he didn't topple over while she was showing him a new tai chi move. "Mr. Rogers would be better equipped to deal with this situation."

"We just want to know someone has your back."

Staring at her, intent on making her point, she said, "Joshua has no training. He's scared of his own shadow. And he is lousy at investigating. He doesn't have my back, Alexa."

Leaning on the table, her friend returned her piercing gaze. "Joshua might not fight or carry a gun, but he doesn't shy away from trouble."

"Are you kidding me? He won't even send the wrong order back at a restaurant."

"He is extremely intelligent and capable of investigating. He's a coroner, Eva. His job is investigation."

She sank back and frowned. There was no point in tossing out her bullshit excuses. Alexa would dismantle each one. "Why him?"

"Who else would we send?"

"I don't need a man as backup."

Alexa nodded. "We know that. Holly is still healing from her last case. She'd die before she admitted it, but she is. Josh isn't there to take care of you, Eva. He's there to give Holly peace of mind. She's worried about you being alone."

Suddenly Holly's insistence made sense. She'd always trusted the HEARTS to take care of themselves before, but her last case had been terrifying and Jack and Holly had both found their lives on the line. Eva could understand how that would shake their lead investigator. Rene was usually the worrywart, the one who warned them about safety and made them wear personal tracers so they could find each other if someone didn't check in. That tracer had saved Holly's life, but Eva could understand how she would start wavering in her conviction that each of the women was more than capable.

They'd gone through too much. All of them. They all had their own scars and burdens, and almost losing Holly had unnerved each one in their own way.

"Has Josh done something to upset you?"

Thoughts of Holly's incident were immediately buried under a surge of a different kind of memory. Josh's arms around her. His scent filling her. The warmth of his body against hers. All those things flashed through her mind, and her heart tripped over itself trying to keep up. She'd woken curled against him the last two mornings. She would have been angry, but she was on *his* side of the bed. She had rolled into him.

He took the intrusion far more graciously than she would have. She would have been angry. He made coffee and scrambled eggs before crashing on the couch to watch a documentary on old FBI files. When they were dating, they had to compromise. He liked documentaries. She liked crime shows. They merged the two, so they were both happy. She had kept watching their show even after they had broken up. Apparently he had, too.

"No," she answered. "He hasn't done anything to upset me."

Alexa tilted her head in that big-sister way of hers. Her eyes were soft but probing and her smile supportive.

Eva sighed. "Stop it."

"What?"

Running a hand over her long hair, she mirrored Alexa and wrapped her hair into a bun and then secured it with one of the many pens she had lined up on the table. "He hasn't upset me. He's been...Josh."

"Sweet and concerned about you?"

Dropping her hands, Eva gawked. "Really?"

A smirk played across Alexa's lips. "You know, he still doesn't quite understand why you two broke up."

"Yes, he does. I told him."

"That's not what I mean. He knows his behavior upset you, but he doesn't really understand why. I tried to explain it to him."

"I *did* explain it to him."

"But not in terms he understood."

"One of his many degrees is in linguistics. I'm confident he understood what I said."

Alexa let out a frustrated sigh as she rolled her head back. "Eva. Don't make me strangle you."

"Strangle him. He's the dick."

Eyeing her, she said, "He's not a dick. He's an incredibly nice guy who is crazy about you."

She pouted a little. Not because Alexa wasn't taking her side but because she was right. "He doesn't trust me."

"He fears for you. Think about it. He deals with dead bodies all day. He's not used to dealing with active criminals. He finds out how the victims died. He's not tracking down who killed them. This is intimidating to him. *You* are intimidating to him."

Frowning, Eva muttered, "Everything is intimidating to Josh."

Alexa gave the sisterly look again. "So maybe the issue isn't that he questions your competency but that you question his."

Eva opened her mouth, about to reject the notion, but then an anvil landed on her head. "He's smart."

"Yes."

"And he"—she scrunched up her face in disgust —"messes with corpses all day."

"Yes."

"He's competent."

"Just in a different way."

Eva glared across the table at Alexa. "What is your point?"

"You said you ended things with Josh because he couldn't handle your line of work. Maybe, Ms. Eva, you couldn't handle his. Nothing about being a coroner screams alpha male, does it? He's not a cop. He's definitely not an adrenaline junkie like law enforcement officials tend to be. He's just sweet, quiet Josh who worries every single day that you're going to get hurt. And you're not used to that. You're used to tough guys. Josh isn't a tough guy."

"No." Recalling how sore he was after their short trip to the gym, she snickered. "He's not."

"But you were attracted to him anyway. For a long time. Why do you think that is?"

Eva didn't answer. She needed to change the subject,

get her focus back on the Jupiter Heights Voyeur case, but something held her fast, staring into Alexa's soft brown eyes.

"Because he wanted more than just a quick lay and a pat on the ass as he left."

That made Eva blink.

"He cares about you. Genuinely. Down to his core. And that terrifies you."

Eva opened her mouth, but no words came out. After a solid four to five seconds of acting like a damn guppy—mouth open, mouth closed, and then open again—she flipped Alexa the bird. "Help me with this case or fuck off."

Alexa rolled her head back and laughed.

Holly marched into the room, grabbing the remote for the flat screen. "Josh is on the news."

"What?" Eva asked as the television came to life.

Eva tuned out the newscaster talking about the horrific murder as she watched Josh in the background, well beyond the yellow tape that had been used to block the scene of a crime.

Alexa gasped, and Eva blinked, finally listening and not just seeing.

"We are being told the victim was just four years old," the woman said.

Eva's heart clenched in her chest. This was a tragedy all around, but she couldn't help thinking how this would impact Josh.

"Did he use a cover story at the condo?" Holly asked.

"*Eva?*"

Blinking, she focused on the team's lead investigator. "Huh?"

She pointed to the television. "Did Josh's cover just get blown?"

"Uh, no. No, we said he was a doctor, but we didn't specify what kind. If anyone asks, we can just tell them he prefers to keep that to himself to avoid questions. We can work around this."

Holly's relief was palpable, but then her frown returned and she focused on the television again. "What the hell is wrong with people?"

Eva couldn't answer that, but as she watched Joshua pushing a gurney with a black body bag to the coroner's vehicle without an ounce of emotion on his face, she thought that she'd been wrong about him all along.

He was a tough guy. He was probably the toughest guy she'd ever known.

Josh slammed the condo door and toed his shoes off, kicking them to the side, not caring if the soles hit and scuffed the gray wall. Gray was a stupid fucking color for a wall anyway. Everything in this condo was stupid. The gray walls, the exposed ductwork, the goddamned windows. And the metal hooks that weren't long enough to hang a fucking coat on.

Giving up, he cursed and threw his coat down. Pissed

at the cooler weather the rain had brought and everything else he could think of.

Marching toward the bedroom, needing a hot shower to wash his day away, he barely glanced over when Eva dropped a folder on the coffee table and eyed him from behind her glasses. Seeing her like that, wearing thick-framed black spectacles that he thought made her even more beautiful, was almost enough to take the edge off his bad mood.

"Are you okay?" she asked.

"Fine." The moment of reprieve was over. Her question reminded him of the toddler he'd spent the afternoon examining. Such a small little body on a long, cold steel table. He didn't care if he was a coroner. He'd never get used to seeing death come to such innocents. Running his fingers through his hair, he continued his trip to the bedroom.

He'd just dug a pair of lounge pants from his dresser drawer when she appeared in the doorway.

"I saw the news," she said quietly. "About the boy killed today. Saw you at the scene."

"I can't talk about it."

"I didn't ask for details."

Slamming one drawer, he opened another. "He was only four years old."

"They arrested his father."

"He's still dead," he said.

He was looking for a T-shirt when she slid her arms around his waist. She hugged him tight, resting her cheek against his back. Though he wanted to push her away and cling to his anger, a wave of warmth washed over him. Stress whooshed out on a breath, and he covered her hands with his.

This.

This was what he missed the most. The peace that Eva brought to his soul on the darkest of days. Whatever he'd done to upset her couldn't possibly be serious enough for her to want to lose this. This had to be worth so much more than her pride. Why couldn't she see that?

"I'm sorry," Eva whispered, as if she'd heard his thoughts.

Josh shook his head. "No. I'm sorry. I don't mean to take my bad day out on you."

"I can handle it," she reassured him.

"But it's not fair."

"Not much in this life is."

Closing his eyes, he dared to turn in her embrace and pull her even closer. She didn't fight his hold as he buried his face in her hair. Her scent filled him, erasing the stench of the brutal death he'd been immersed in earlier. But the images... Those weren't so easily forgotten.

"He smashed his little skull with a hammer, Eva."

"Shhh," she soothed as he choked on the statement and hugged him even tighter.

Warmth spread across his shirt, just a small spot where the material absorbed a tear from her eye. Eva wasn't a crier. The only time he'd ever seen tears in her eyes were cases—his or those from HEARTS—that involved children. Those cases ate at them, both of them.

Josh probably would have held her there forever, losing himself in the feel of her, but she leaned back.

"Are you hungry?"

"No."

"Okay," she said softly. "Start a bath. I'll grab you a drink."

He didn't move as she left him. He couldn't. He felt hollowed out. This day had drained every ounce of strength he had. He was still standing where she'd left him when she returned with two drinks in her hands. Instead of the sarcastic retort that he would usually get from her, she offered a sympathetic smile as she bypassed him and went into the bathroom.

The tub in the condo wasn't as large as the one they used to submerge into at her apartment, but it was big enough for him to stretch out a bit more than in the average bath. By the time he leaned against the doorjamb, she was sitting on the tiled edge, testing the temperature as water poured from the spigot.

"Jack's right," he said without thinking. "I do love you."

She didn't respond. The rushing water had drowned out his words.

He considered repeating his confession but thought maybe it was best if she didn't hear. The last thing he needed to deal with tonight was Eva dancing around telling him she didn't feel the same.

She looked over her shoulder then, offered him a supportive smile, and then returned her attention to the bath she was running for him. She pressed the button to start the jets, and he crossed the room. Kneeling beside her, he rested his hands on her thigh. Her bright eyes met his, and he smiled. The questions in her eyes were clear, but she didn't put her guard up. That was a big step for them. For both of them.

Usually she tossed sarcasm at him to keep an emotional mile of distance, to keep him on the other side of the wall. She was letting him in now, likely because she knew his soul was aching from the hell he'd seen. Turning him away would be cruel. Eva was tough, hard when she needed to be, but she could never be cruel.

Part of him wanted to shove his way into the door she was opening for him, but that would cause her to shut down. "Thanks," he said. "I appreciate you taking care of me."

She ruffled his hair, but the motion was lacking the usual teasing. This had a caring, protective vibe to it. "Always, Joshie."

Even the dreaded nickname sounded loving in that moment and brought a bit more peace to his heart.

"I'll make some dinner, okay?"

Standing, he took a step back to give her room. "Sounds good. Thanks." Putting his hand to her arm, he stopped her before she left him alone and put his lips to her forehead. He cupped the back of her head and stole one more sweet moment that he could commit to his memory before this passed and they went back to their normal lives, pretending their feelings didn't run nearly as deep as they both knew they did.

Once alone, he sat on the edge where she'd been watching the water fall into the tub. The movement mesmerized him, the sound of the jet motors hypnotizing him. He stared until a knock on the door broke his trance.

"Josh? Can I come in?"

"Sure," he answered.

Eva opened the door and peered in as if afraid of what she'd see. Her face fell into a frown when she spied him. "I thought you'd be soaking by now. I was checking to see if you needed another beer."

Closing the door behind her, she crossed the bathroom and turned off the water. It had risen so high, it'd likely overflow if he climbed in. Reaching in, she turned the plug and let the water start draining. Kneeling in front of him, she looked up and searched his eyes as if she could see his soul. Without asking, she reached for the buttons of his shirt, releasing them until she could push the material off his shoulders. After tossing it aside, she replugged the drain, tugged his undershirt off, and then pulled him to his feet.

She gripped his waistband, tugged, and then grinned. "You can handle this part on your own."

He did. He released his belt and pushed his pants down as she turned off the overhead light, leaving only the vanity lights on a timer to soften the mood in the bathroom. He climbed into the tub, hissing a bit at the temperature, which was a little hotter than he would have liked, but he didn't complain. He sank down, leaning back, and closed his eyes.

He didn't open them again until he felt her climbing into the other end of the tub. Just like she used to do. The lights were so dim and she moved so quickly he could barely make out her body, but he'd memorized how she looked naked the first time he'd seen her without clothing. He could clearly remember the light triangle of hair over her pubic bone. The light pink areolas around nipples that reacted to the lightest of touches. He had no doubt they were pebbled now, hard against the current the jets were creating, just like they used to harden under the flicking of his tongue.

She grinned when he finally lifted his gaze to hers. He couldn't see her breasts through the shadows playing on the water, but he certainly had been staring hard enough to try. He smiled, too, just a slightly embarrassed grin.

"Sorry. Men and boobs."

Leaning forward a bit, she made a show of peering at his crotch, though he guessed her view was just as obstructed as his. "Sorry," she said, raising her eyes to his. "Women and cocks."

They both chuckled as she sat back.

"This isn't an invitation to sex," she said. "That would be a huge mistake for both of us. But I know how much being like this helps you, and I want to help you."

The weight of his burden returned, but it wasn't nearly as heavy as it had been even ten minutes prior. He didn't need sex. She knew that. He just needed her and their undeniable emotional connection. Feeling her close to him was all he needed.

Running his hand over her shin, he soaked in the feel of her as much as he soaked in the heat of the water and the soft pounding of the water jets. Nothing could ever take away the horror of what he'd seen, but having Eva this close, taking care of him as only she could, was the closest he'd ever get to making peace with it.

9

Sipping her coffee, Eva tried to block out the sound of Josh stirring eggs behind her. The continuous clink of the fork against the bowl echoed through the condo and grated on her nerves. She hadn't slept well the night before, and no amount of coffee was going to take the irritation from her at the moment. "Josh," she stated as kindly as she could. "They're ready."

He stopped his rhythmic motion and blinked at her as if he needed time to digest her words. "Sorry. I was...elsewhere."

Easing her cup down, she softened her approach. "You okay?"

His smile seemed genuine. Sad but genuine. "Yeah. Thanks again for getting me through last night."

Mention of the evening before sent her thoughts reeling. After his bath, they'd sat at the table in their PJs eating dinner, engaging in quiet conversation instead of their new habit of hitting the condo's gym before unwinding for the evening. After they'd crawled into bed, he tossed and turned until she'd curled into him. He'd turned, pulled her against him, and they'd fallen asleep in a tangle of arms and legs.

They'd woken up that way the last few days, shrugged it off, and moved on. This morning, however, his heat seeped into her skin and touched her in a way she hadn't permitted before. Ever before. That should be a good thing, right?

She didn't understand the cloud that had hovered over her since waking with his arms around her. No. That wasn't accurate. She knew *exactly* what was bothering her.

He'd said words they'd never said before. He might have thought she hadn't heard him tell her that he loved her as she'd run his bath, but she had. She'd heard him clearly. She hadn't responded because...because maybe he hadn't meant it. Maybe his heart was broken from the death of a child and he was hurting and needed to feel connected to someone and she was there. Maybe he was emotional from the pain he'd had to shove down to do his job.

She knew how easy it was to say things when the brain was coming off an adrenaline high. She knew better than to trust the words that came from his mouth when he was so upset.

But damned if she didn't want to. She'd left him to his

bath and stared out the window thinking *what if*. What if he *had* meant it? What if Alexa was right and it wasn't Josh's fear for her safety that made her break up with him? What if everything she ever wanted was right there for the taking and she'd walked away because of fear and pride and a million other stupid things?

She kept a wall between her and the outside world, simply because she had to. She couldn't have been a cop or a PI and seen some of the things she'd seen without having a tough exterior. But maybe Josh had been right when he'd told her so many times that it was okay to let him in. She almost had before he'd started freaking out about something happening to her and started asking her to stop doing her job. A job she loved. A job that defined her.

After he'd dozed off and started softly snoring, Eva had rolled Alexa's point over in her mind. Eva was scared. Terrified. She'd let Josh in once, and he'd hurt her. The fact that that hadn't been his intent didn't take the sting away. She was used to being underestimated and mocked by other men, but coming from Josh, that lack of faith in her had felt like a hot knife slicing her heart. She didn't want to feel that pain again.

Playing house for a few days had reminded her how good the good times had been but also made her recall the slap she felt every time he suggested she do something different with her life. Or take a different approach to solving crimes.

She'd accepted him for the geeky *Star Trek* groupie

that he was. Or so she'd thought. But once again, she had to consider that maybe Alexa was right. Maybe Eva hadn't been as open to Josh as she'd thought. She'd done plenty of her own nudging to get him to do things she was more interested in.

The man had taken a knife-throwing class, for fuck's sake. She was 99.9 percent certain he never would have done that if she hadn't cajoled him into it. No. If it'd been up to Josh, they would have gone to Comic-Con dressed like aliens or superheroes. She'd never done that for him. She'd never given him an inch. She'd always insisted that they compromise, but now, standing back, it certainly seemed like Josh was the only one who had.

He'd been surprised when she'd been so quick to take care of him, and she couldn't help but wonder if that was because she'd been so lacking in that department before. She wasn't a natural nurturer. She knew that. She definitely could have given more and taken less. She could have been more sensitive to his needs. Being there for him last night had felt so right. They hadn't crossed the line she'd put into place, but even so, she'd felt more connected to him in that bathtub sitting in silence as he processed and healed than she'd felt any time they'd been fucking.

Goddamn it. Why did this have to be so messy? Why weren't relationships easy? Why couldn't she be a PI and he be a geeky coroner and that be enough for both of them? It *should* be enough for both of them. She shouldn't need him to be more, and he shouldn't need her to be less to meet in the middle. And she sure as hell shouldn't be so scared of taking care of him when he needed her.

"Do you want eggs?" Josh asked, breaking into her stream of thought.

Eggs? She blinked as he'd done before. "Uh. No. Thanks. You know, I was thinking," she said before she could stop herself. "We should start binge-watching those superhero movies you've been trying to force me to sit through."

His eyes lit. "*The Avengers?* You want to watch *The Avengers?*" His smile remained, but the brightness in his eyes dimmed. "You don't have to do that, Eva. I'm okay. Really."

She shrugged. "No, I mean. There's a new one coming out soon, right?" Seemed like there was always a new one coming out soon. "You always tell me I need to get caught up before the next one. So catch me up."

"You don't have to—"

"Bring home a pizza. Something spicy and greasy. Maybe some wings." She'd need the indigestion to help her through endless hours of him excitedly dissecting every detail of the movies.

His excitement returned. "Done."

"I'll wear a Batman T-shirt for the occasion."

Josh visibly winced at her geek faux pas. "No, that's DC..." He smirked, trailing off before he could inform her about the ongoing DC vs Marvel battle, when she chuckled. "You knew that. I'm impressed."

"Just because I don't watch superhero movies doesn't mean I live under a rock, Joshie. Cook your eggs, or you'll be late for work." She hadn't meant the words to sound so sweet, but the affection in her tone was undeniable.

He blushed and smiled but had the sense to keep his thoughts, whatever they had been, to himself as he dumped the egg-and-milk mixture into a hot pan. "What are you doing today?"

"There is something off about Neal Price's wife. I need to find her and figure out what that is exactly."

"What are you thinking it is?"

"She is definitely unhappy. I'd like to try to pinpoint why."

"And what does that have to do with our voyeur?"

"My gut is telling me Neal Price and Shane Tremant are in this thing together. Maybe Tremant strong-armed Price. He's definitely the alpha between the two. I'm wondering if Mrs. Price is less than thrilled with what the men are up to."

He scraped a spatula across the hot pan to stir his eggs. "Can you imagine finding out your spouse is a pervert?"

"Maybe she's always known." Shrugging, she snagged an apple. "She drives her daughter to school about this time every morning. I'm going to try to catch her coming home and get a better read on her. I'll see you later." She turned toward the door and then stopped and looked back at him. "Try not to let the job get in your head today."

"I'll try. Thanks."

She rolled her head back as she waited for the elevator to answer her press of the button. "Did I seriously suggest watching *The Avengers*? Man, that's gonna suck."

The bell dinged. Thankfully the car was empty and the ride to the first floor smooth. Sitting in a corner of the lobby, flipping through a magazine and chomping on her apple, she kept the majority of her attention on the building's main entrance.

Eva jumped up as soon as Brenda Price walked in, looking like an unamused princess in perfectly cut Victoria's Secret sweats with a Gucci bag hanging off her arm. Big sunglasses with a logo on the side that Eva didn't recognize blocked out the morning sun and covered a good portion of Brenda's face. The messy bun on top of her head bounced with each borderline stomp the woman made. She stopped at the elevator, pressed the button, and started staring at her phone as she waited.

With her so deeply distracted, Eva stepped behind her without being noticed. When the elevator opened, she stepped in. "Good morning, Mrs. Price. How are you today?"

Brenda's face didn't move. Eva wondered if it could. Her skin was plumped and stiff from the side effects of her latest measures to stay young. This process baffled Eva; the woman's background check put her at forty-two. How much age damage could she have to hide?

"Have fun shopping with Tiffany?"

The bitterness in Brenda's voice was a verbal sucker

punch. Eva forced her smile to stay firm, as if she hadn't heard the anger. "It was great. She certainly knows all the best places to shop."

"Yes. She does get around."

Oh. That was a double entendre if she'd ever heard one. Eva again acted as if she hadn't noticed but would definitely look into that later. "If you aren't busy, maybe we could grab breakfast. Or lunch. I'd love to—"

"I know who you are and why you're here, Ms. Thompson. Cut the neighborly bullshit."

Damn it, Price. She cursed the man who'd hired her. No one, absolutely no one, was supposed to know her real motives for being there. But Eva was more than happy to drop the perky persona. She was exhausted from the sprightly facade she'd been layering on the last few days.

Brenda tugged the strap of her bag onto her shoulder. The lights of the elevator shone through her sunglass lenses just enough that Eva saw the dramatic eye roll. "The least you can do is not try to rub my nose in it."

Eva paused at that statement. Maybe Brenda Price didn't know the real reason she was there. "I'm not sure what you mean."

She smirked—as much as her muscle-paralyzing injections would allow. "Don't play innocent with me."

"I'm not."

The doors slid open, and she stepped out. Turning before the doors closed, she said, "If you don't, you'll find out soon enough. You are just their type."

Whoa! Eva put her hand on the door before it could close. She stepped out and followed Brenda. She wasn't going to let that comment fall. "Who? What are you talking about?"

She spun on her heel toward her condo door, but Eva moved around her to block her way.

"Brenda?"

Eva eased her imposing stance and looked over her shoulder at Neal Price as he approached the confrontation.

"What's going on here?" he asked, looking from Eva to Brenda and back again.

Brenda managed a smile. "Your new friend was inviting me to breakfast. Unfortunately, I'm busy today. Aren't I, Neal?"

He frowned at her but didn't respond.

Brenda smirked at Eva. "He thinks Cody's in some kind of trouble. She's sixteen, but I've been delegated to helicopter-parenting like she's a toddler playing with mousetraps."

"She's getting money from somewhere."

"Taking lessons from her father, no doubt." She practically stomped to their condo door and disappeared behind it.

Turning his attention to Eva, Price scowled. "What was that about?"

"You tell me. She seems to think there's a reason I'm here. One that has a lot more to do with my appearance than finding out who put a camera in Wendi Carter's condo."

His eyes bulged. "Did you tell her about that?"

"Of course not."

"Keep it that way. I paid you to figure this out and stop it before it happens to someone else. Where are you on that?"

"I bet it'd be a lot easier if the security cameras monitoring your hallways recorded footage that could actually be useful."

He tensed his jaw and narrowed his eyes. "Stay away from my wife, Ms. Thompson. She has nothing to do with this."

"She's upset about something."

"*Not* about this. Leave her alone."

"Hey," she called when he started around her. She glanced around and then whispered, "You've been working on upgrading the security for a few days. What's the company name? I'll reach out to them."

"I'll take care of it." He left her standing there in the hallway, scowling and even more suspicious of him than she'd been when she'd decided to question his wife in the first place.

What kind of HOA president didn't want reliable security? She was beginning to think his lack of interest in upgrading the system was more about protecting himself than his fellow residents. When he'd come to HEARTS, he was so concerned about defending Jupiter Heights's reputation. Maybe he was more concerned with making sure he continued to get away with whatever it was that he and Shane Tremant were covering up.

Facing the closed door, the one that shielded the Prices from her suspicious gaze, she debated just how much Brenda Price knew and the best way to get her talking.

Josh dropped the pizza box on the counter because Eva had photos spread across the kitchen table. She wasn't dressed in comfy binge-watching clothes. She was still dressed for work in black slacks, a white blouse, and her gun in the holster on the table. He wasn't trying to pout, but he should have known she'd forget their plans. He'd spent all day looking forward to sitting next to her on the sofa, watching his favorite movies with her. He'd hoped she had too, but she was engrossed in her case.

"Stop scowling," she chastised. "I'll clean this up in a minute."

"What is this, exactly?"

She joined him at the counter and flipped the box top back. Closing her eyes, she inhaled deeply. "God, that smells good." She dropped two slices onto a plate. "I talked to Brenda Price this morning. She *confronted* me is a more accurate description."

He sat on a barstool and immediately started plucking toppings off the slice he'd chosen. "About what?"

"Why do you always get green peppers? You never eat them."

"Because you like them. Why did she confront you?"

A strange mix of what looked like confusion and awe played across her face before she wiped her hands on a napkin. "She said the only reason I'm here is because I'm *their* type."

"Whose type?"

"She didn't get a chance to answer that. Her husband interrupted us, and she stormed off. Then he warned me to stay away from her. But it got me thinking."

"About?"

Sinking onto a barstool, she narrowed her eyes. "Have you noticed how the majority of the residents here are single, fair-haired females? Brenda Price is the only tanned brunette woman I've seen around here. I've spent all day wandering the grounds, being neighborly"—she rolled her eyes to show her displeasure—"and I've confirmed something I hadn't noticed before. There is very little variety here. The women all look the same."

"Like you."

"Just like me. And do you know who has final say in who lives here? Neal Price."

His stomach knotted around the pizza in his gut. He had a bad feeling about that. He didn't like the idea of someone handpicking Eva for some sinister motive.

Let Eva do her job, Joshua. "Another red flag for Price, then?"

"Yes. It is. He was surprised when I told him you

would be moving in with me. I didn't think much about it because he hired *me*, not you, to live here. I just told him for safety's sake we always work in pairs. He didn't say anything about it, but...maybe that shock was disappointment?" She leaned on the counter and bit her plump bottom lip as she lifted her eyes to his. "I hate to do this."

He sighed. "You're heading to HEARTS?"

"I asked Holly to meet with me. Not just about this; we need to find out the name of the security company manning those cameras. Price doesn't want to let me in on that. She didn't have any time available this afternoon, but she texted me about fifteen minutes ago. She doesn't have much time, but I want her to see these pictures and go over my notes. I'll be back in plenty of time to squeeze in part one of our nerd fest."

He smiled when she did. "Yeah. I mean, you're here to stop a pervert. So...go stop a pervert."

"How was your day?"

"Better."

"Really?"

He could tell her all about it, but that would distract her from her case, and as much as he loved being here with her all the time, he wanted this case to be over. The uneasy feeling in his stomach was telling him the longer she stayed in this building, the more danger she was going to be in. Job or not, he didn't like it and wanted her out of Jupiter Heights. "Really. Go. I'm sure Holly wants to get home to Jack."

"Yeah. Thanks for the pizza. It was really good."

He could have eaten more, watched something on Netflix while he waited for her, but as soon as she left him alone, the condo seemed far too empty. He put the pizza away and debated taking a shower. Standing in the bathroom doorway just reminded him how he'd finally accepted and professed his love for her. Knowing she wouldn't be able to hear him as water filled the tub.

Chickenshit.

He paced the condo for a few more minutes before putting on some of the workout clothes he'd bought after he'd decided to take advantage of the Jupiter Heights gym while they lived there. Wearing baggy shorts and a moisture-wicking T-shirt to keep his body temperature regulated as he exerted his barely there muscles.

He'd just walked into the small space crammed full of machines when he spotted Price and Tremant hanging out. Literally hanging out. They weren't exercising. Just standing around the equipment, talking quietly. As soon as Josh walked in, they put a bit more space between them and acted like he hadn't interrupted an intense conversation. Neal Price waved, asked how he was doing, but neither showed any genuine interest in him. Instead they went back to lifting weights—Price spotting Tremant.

Josh hopped on the elliptical, the closest bit of equipment he dared to utilize, and put buds into his ears. However, when he fiddled with his phone, instead of finding music, he opened the recorder he sometimes used as a backup while making notes in autopsy or at a crime scene. Pulling the earbud plug out just enough to disengage it so the microphone would pick up external noise, he started moving the steps on the elliptical.

He occasionally glanced at the men in the mirror. They had stopped lifting and were once again muttering quietly. Josh had no idea if the phone would pick up their voices, but he sure as hell hoped so, given the torture he was enduring to capture whatever nugget he could. His legs started burning two minutes in. He reminded himself that the buildup of lactic acid was causing the discomfort and his muscles weren't really on fire, but that logic didn't make him want to push though.

Okay. It was time. He seriously needed to start working out. Really working out. Not coming down to the gym when he was bored and tinkering with the equipment or lifting a hand weight a few times to appease the part of him that was demanding he start taking care of himself.

If he lived through this, he vowed as he wiped sweat off his brow, it was time to get serious. He checked the resistance, not once but twice, confirming he was working on the easiest level. Even so, sweat was coating his skin faster than the moisture wick could keep up with. His temperature and his breath increased to a pant as his lungs tried to keep up with the oxygen needs of his body.

Dear Lord. He was going to die.

Finally, after what must have been an hour, the door to the gym closed with a loud click and Josh was alone. He nearly collapsed onto the elliptical panel when his gaze fell on the clock.

Six minutes. He'd only been on the damned machine for six minutes. He didn't believe it. He stepped onto the floor on shaky legs and turned off the recorder. Sitting on a bench, he rested his elbows on his knees and pushed the earbud plug all the way in. Restarting the recording, he focused on slowing his breathing. The voices in the background were unintelligible for the most part. Every now and then, if he squinted his eyes and really strained to hear, Josh could catch a word or two.

"I'm telling you. She knows," one of them said.

"Don't blow this," the other said a few moments later.

Then: "Just be cool. She can't be that smart."

"Hi, Joshua," a voice said, loud enough to break through his concentration.

Josh glanced up. Melly...he couldn't remember her last name...wriggled her fingers at him. He was all too familiar with how difficult it was to get away from her. Eva had mentioned it every time they saw her after the potluck.

He didn't have time to get stuck in pointless conversation. He had to get his phone to Eva to see if she could pull more information off the device. He smiled, waved, and started for the door. He was nearly there before he spotted the wipes intended to keep the equipment clean. He hesitated but then gave in to the need to clean his sweat off the elliptical. Plucking out one lemon-scented disposable cloth, he wiped the handles, tossed the wipe on his way out the door, and dialed Eva's phone as he rushed to the locker room to grab his bag.

"Are you and Holly still at the office?"

"Yeah."

"Don't leave. I have something for you. See you in about fifteen."

After ending the call, he tucked his phone into the deep pocket of his bag. He didn't need to run up to the condo; he had his car keys with his other belongings. Lifting his arm just a few inches, he sniffed his pits to make sure he didn't stink. He still smelled like the Acqua di Parma Colonia Club he'd splashed on earlier in the day. The hints of lavender and citrus had faded but still overwhelmed any chemical scents from work or release of hormones from his mini-exercise routine.

He started whistling an old Prince tune as he silently congratulated himself on a job well done. He was about to reach out to the locker room door when it slammed open. The door cracked against his face, smashing his nose before he had a chance to lift his hand in a defensive measure.

His cartilage made a *crunch* sound as bright white starbursts filled his eyes. He diagnosed his injury as a nasal fracture before he even looked up. When he did, he groaned, anticipating the next hit moments before the door smacked his face again.

This time he had his hand over his face, but that didn't stop the pain from shooting through him. He stumbled back, closed his eyes, and dropped to his knees. Warm fluid filled his palm. He didn't have to check. He knew it was blood.

Before he could confront whoever was on the other

side of the door for breaking his nose, he was shoved onto his side and patted down, and then his bag was snatched from his hand. The door clicked closed behind his attacker. Blinking hard, Josh looked up, trying to assess what had just happened.

10

EVA WAS GOING to kill Josh. She was going to wrap her fingers around that long neck of his and squeeze until there was no life left in him. She'd told him this was dangerous. When he hadn't shown up like he'd promised and then hadn't answered her texts or calls, she and Holly had rushed to the condo to find him leaning over the bathroom sink, his face swollen and bruised as he tried to wash away dried blood.

Damn it. She'd told him a hundred times he couldn't take care of himself. She'd told Holly they were putting him in harm's way. And there he sat at the dining room table with his face bashed in as Holly examined his injury. She'd done two tours in the Army, and knew plenty of first aid, but not enough to be dealing with whatever was going on with Josh's quickly distorting face.

"I'm taking him to the ER," Eva said.

"I'm okay," Josh insisted, his voice sounding cartoonishly high-pitched from the inflammation pinching off his nostrils.

Holly lowered her hands from his puffy cheeks. "I agree with Eva. It's definitely broken. You should get it set by a physician."

"I am a physician."

"For corpses," Eva snapped.

Instead of acknowledging her comment, he touched his nose but instantly flinched and jerked away from his own contact. She rolled her eyes, shoved herself from where she'd been leaning against the counter, and opened the freezer. He'd used the only ice pack she'd put in there when they moved in. It had thawed too much to be useful, but there were several bags of frozen vegetables.

"Tells us one more time," Holly pushed. "What happened?"

"I was in the gym. Price and Tremant were acting odd. I clearly interrupted a conversation. I hit record on my phone and—"

"In the locker room, Joshua," Eva barked, selecting a bag of peas. "What happened in the locker room?"

"I'd just gotten to the door when someone shoved it open and hit my face. I thought it was an accident, but then he hit me again. I fell to my knees, holding my face, and he came in. He patted me down and then stole my bag with my keys and phone inside. I was too dazed to follow him."

"Did you get a look at him?" Holly asked. "Even a

glimpse to give you an idea of how tall he was or how much he weighed?"

He accepted the frozen veggies Eva held out to him. "No, I guess I didn't."

"I want your locks changed tonight," Holly told Eva.

She gnawed at her lip, rolling Wendi's interview through her mind. "Wendi had lost her keys. Only temporarily, but long enough for someone to make an impression to get a copy made. That took planning. This attack on Josh doesn't seem well planned. I'm guessing he took Josh's keys to gain access to our condo and put in cameras. Once he does, we have him. Busted."

"If this really is Tremant, as you suspect, and Price is working with him, they know better than to put cameras in your condo," Holly said.

"Do they? Or are they so cocky they'd try it anyway?"

Holly pushed herself up from the table and yanked off the latex gloves she'd been wearing to examine Josh's face. "Josh was attacked, Eva. Violently."

"I bet you anything that's what Tremant and Price were plotting in the gym. How to get keys to this condo and install cameras to find out what I know. As soon as they saw Josh in the gym, they saw their chance and went for it."

Holly started shaking her head before Eva finished. "Why would Price have to attack Josh to get the keys? He likely kept a set when he moved you in."

Eva frowned, hating Holly's logic. Before she could

come up with a likely reason, Alexa opened the condo door and eased it closed behind her.

Eva was certain she knew the answer to her question from the look on her teammate's face, but she had to ask anyway. "Find anything?"

"Nope. A custodian wiped down the scene before we got there."

"And once again I say, how *fucking* convenient." Eva's hard tone matched the set of her jaw. She focused on Holly and listed her circumstantial evidence, ticking the points off on her fingers. "Price lost the cameras, hired shitty security, and now his staff is cleaning up the scene of an assault before we can get a look?"

Alexa winced as she looked at Josh's rapidly blackening eyes. "But he hired us."

"Because he doesn't think we can catch him."

Holly tossed the used gloves into the trash can and pumped soap into her palm. "Wouldn't be the first time a man naturally assumed we were incompetent because of our genitalia."

Eva cocked her brows. "And it won't be the first time we've proved a man wrong."

"Or the last," Alexa added.

"What are you going to do?" Holly asked.

Eva tapped her fingers on the counter. "How many spycams do we have in the office?"

"About six," Alexa told her as Holly washed her hands.

"That's more than enough to catch a liar in a lie," Eva

said, already determining the best place to put her own hidden cameras.

Josh hissed in pain as he put the peas to his face.

"I'll grab them tomorrow after our morning meeting." Snatching up her car keys, Eva helped Josh stand. "Come on, Boy Wonder. Let's go get your pretty little face fixed."

Though he was several inches taller, Josh rested his arm on her shoulder and accepted her support as they headed for the elevator. She kept her eyes out, scanning the area, more to avoid answering neighbors' questions than out of any fear they were in danger.

Word spread like wildfire around here, and she wanted to maintain positive control over whatever the story was that they'd give for Josh's condition. That would be easier if they could get out of the building without being spotted.

Relief washed over her when they made it all the way to her sedan and she was able to ease him into the passenger seat without being forced to come up with a lie. Once she was behind the steering wheel and backing out of her assigned parking spot, though, she glanced over. "We need a cover story."

"Basketball," he said. "I got elbowed playing basketball."

She shrugged. "Good enough. Have you ever played basketball?"

"Once. Jack invited me because someone on his team was sick."

"That's nice."

"I sucked so bad they never invited me back."

She chuckled. "Not everyone can be an athlete, Josh."

He dropped his head back and moaned. "I'm sorry."

"Why?"

"Because you're right. I'm not cut out for this. I was trying to help."

Her heart tripped and broke a little at the defeat in his voice. Yeah, sure, she had said that. And, yeah, she was right, but she didn't like hearing him sound so down on himself. "You did good."

"No, I didn't."

"You tried good." She glanced over at him and smiled when he turned his face to her. Chuckling, she put her hand on his, squeezing tight. "I'm sorry I was snappy. I don't like seeing you hurt."

"I know."

Sighing, she focused on the drive to the hospital. She'd get his face fixed first. Then she'd work on making sure this never happened to him again.

Josh eased onto the sofa with Eva's help. His injury hadn't been serious enough for the ER staff to rush, which meant they'd spent over two hours at the hospital. But his nose was set, and he had some extra-strength aspirin to help with the pain. Rolling his head back, he closed his eyes against the exhaustion and throbbing that pounded his face with each beat of his heart.

"I should put you to bed," Eva said gently.

Thankfully she was aware of how much his head was aching and had taken pity on him. She'd kept her voice soft and driven with more care than he'd ever known her to. Nurture wasn't a word he'd attribute to Eva most days, but she'd been hyperaware of his condition since arriving at the ER. At first she'd been angry, as if he had asked to get hurt, but then she'd calmed down and started showing some sympathy.

His dad used to act that way, too. Once when he was about eight, Josh decided to build a lab in the backyard. His dad called it a "treehouse," but it wasn't; it was a *scientific laboratory*. Josh had barely gotten through cutting his first board when he dropped a handsaw. The sharp teeth caught and sliced his calf open. He'd fallen, holding his bleeding leg and screaming for his mom to help him. His dad had been so angry, Josh thought he surely must have ruined the tool he'd been using.

Later, though, his mother explained that his dad didn't handle worrying well. Instead of panicking, he got angry. Not angry at the person who was hurt—Josh, in that case —but angry at the world for allowing someone he loved to be injured. Once the apprehension eased, he wasn't angry anymore.

Just like Eva.

She'd been worried when she'd realized he'd been attacked. She'd been terrified when she saw his face bloodied. She'd been angry at the world for hurting him. If she hadn't been, she wouldn't have stood by the ER bed, checking her watch, wondering what was taking the doctor so long. Wondering if anyone understood that Josh was in pain. Chastising him, more than once, for getting hurt in the first place.

She'd been scared. That made his chest blossom with warmth. Even if she didn't express herself well.

"Why are you smiling?" Eva asked, pulling him back to the living room. "You look like my Krav Maga class used you for practice."

His smile widened as he patted the sofa. "Come here."

She hesitated before sitting next to him. Once she did, he covered her clutched hands with one of his.

"I'm okay, Eva."

"I know. The doctor said—"

"Eva," he said with gentle authority, something he rarely asserted with her. "I'm okay."

She closed her eyes and let out a slow breath. "I'm glad."

"I didn't mean to worry you."

Lifting her brows as she pinned him with her gaze, she said, "This is why I didn't want you here, Josh. It could be dangerous. You aren't used to that."

He nodded. "I know. I get it now. But I'm not leaving you here alone."

"You're starting self-defense classes as soon as I can get you in. Not just for this case but because you should know how to take care of yourself."

The role reversal here wasn't lost on Josh. He, as the man, should be having this conversation with her, but Eva

—as she tended to be—was ahead of him in that area. Her brown belt in the same martial arts the military used would have prevented this from happening to her. She had been right all along, not that he should be surprised. She could take care of herself. He couldn't. And that needed to change. "I agree."

"Also, I'm teaching you how to shoot. No argument," she demanded before he could challenge her. "I'll take you to the range, and we'll find a handgun you are comfortable with."

Instead of repeating his dislike for guns—as a coroner, he was far too familiar with the damage they could do—he squeezed her hands. "Did you look to see if any cameras had been placed since we left?" he whispered.

"Not yet."

"Go ahead. I'm fine."

She held his gaze for several breaths before heading into the bedroom. He sat on the sofa while she went through her routine of scanning for heat signatures and then using an infrared camera, making certain they weren't being recorded. When she put her camera down, she held her hand out to him.

"Come on, Joshie." She said the nickname with affection instead of her usual acrimony.

He accepted her extended hand and stood slowly so as not to unsettle his head. He brushed his hand over her hair. "Thanks, Eva...ie."

She snickered. "That doesn't even sound right."

"Neither does Joshie, but I don't correct you."

"Anymore," they said in unison. The moment made him smile while she let out a little laugh.

"Let's get you to bed," she whispered.

Something in the air shifted around them, something sparked, something felt too familiar. He used to stand this close to her all the time. He used to dip his head down the few inches that parted them and kiss her. She used to respond.

However, when he pulled her to close the distance between them, she turned her face at the last moment and his lips brushed her cheek. His heart shattered under the weight of crushing disappointment. Resting his head to hers, he considered apologizing, but he didn't want to. Because he wasn't sorry. He was sad that she didn't reciprocate his desire, but he wasn't sorry that he'd tried.

Eva audibly exhaled in what he was certain was frustration. He couldn't blame her, really. Just the night before, as they'd sat naked in the bathtub, she'd told him it would be a mistake to have sex. How could he think kissing her would somehow not be an error in her mind?

But then she surprised him.

Fisting his T-shirt, she held him in place as she turned enough to claim his mouth. Not in the soft and seductive way he had intended, but in a possessive kiss that reminded him that she would never give an inch unless she wanted to. Her lips crushed against his before parting enough for her tongue to dart across his bottom lip. A moment after bringing the flesh to life with her touch, she sank her teeth into it with a teasing bite that had always led to so much more.

Sliding one hand up his chest, over his shoulder, and into his hair, she tugged him closer so she could deepen the kiss on her terms. He didn't complain. He put his hands to her hips, brought her body against his, and let her have control of their mouths. She could dominate him as she wanted. She could set whatever pace she wanted. He didn't mind at all.

Other than sliding his arms around her and pressing his erection into her stomach, he didn't exert an ounce of power. After another thorough brushing of her tongue against his, she pushed him back and stared into his eyes. The kiss was brief but intense, just as the intimate stage of their relationship had been. She panted, licked her lip, and released her hold on his head as she stepped back.

For a moment he thought the fire in her eyes was going to lead to something more than a hot kiss. Maybe she was going to toss him down and tear his clothes off. He was certain the idea played across her mind. But she didn't act on it. She took another step back, putting more space between them.

"Go to bed, Joshua," she insisted. "You need your rest."

Though he was disappointed that she wouldn't take advantage of his weakened state, he couldn't deny how happy he was at this little turn of events. His lip twitched, but he managed to suppress his excited smile. "Yes, ma'am."

He walked into the bathroom and stopped in front of the mirror, not even seeing his wound. When he'd offered to stay with Eva, he'd never imagined they'd somehow find themselves on the path to getting back together. He had hoped on some level but never allowed himself to believe it. They were *this* close now. He could sense it.

Jealousy. Hot baths. Cuddling as they fell asleep. A hot kiss.

None of those things would have happened if they weren't leading to something bigger. He wasn't going to push Eva, that never worked with her, but he'd be persistent. He'd stay the course. And, if push came to shove, he'd make it a point to run into Courtney.

11

THE MORNING MEETING started just as Sam sashayed into the conference room. Nobody could possibly walk on those heels. Sashaying was the only option. Which was completely unprofessional for a staff member of a private investigation agency. Why the hell did Holly allow that?

Eva tried to tamp down the irritation she felt. Sam wasn't to blame for her foul mood. Eva had done that all on her own. She'd kissed Josh. Why had she done that? That was stupid. So stupid. She'd had to stay up late to ensure he was asleep before she slipped into the bed they were sharing. Then she'd woken up early, tiptoed her way through getting ready, and said good-bye to him as if she hadn't intentionally timed her departure to coincide with the alarm on his phone.

She'd spent the rest of the morning fighting the urge to text and ask how he was doing. He was a grown man. He could take care of himself. He didn't need her.

But he kind of did. He had obviously appreciated her taking care of him the other night when he'd come home from work so upset. And then he'd said that he loved her, and she'd pretended she hadn't heard him.

She still didn't understand why she had done that. Why hadn't she just acknowledged his words? That would have been easier. She should have turned and asked if he'd meant it or if he was simply upset and was seeking comfort. But putting him on the spot like that wouldn't have gotten her an honest answer. He would have felt bad for being caught in an emotional lie and stuttered his way around answering her. She would have blown up and stormed off, and things would be even messier than they were post-passionate kiss.

God, she hated how everything always got so messy. This should be cut and dry. Black and white. Or easy-peasy, lemon squeezy, as Josh would say with his ridiculously chipper outlook on life.

A smile threatened to twitch at the corner of her mouth, but Eva forced it away. She should text him. Check on him. Make sure he'd gotten off to work okay. Like she should have done instead of rushing out of the condo like a chickenshit.

She blinked when an elbow dug into her side. Looking at Sam, she glared, demanding an explanation for the assault with her hard stare.

"Eva, are you okay?" Holly asked.

Shit. Everyone was staring at her.

Because she was at the morning meeting and was

supposed to be listening to case reports and offering feedback and suggestions to her teammates. She'd been too caught up in her personal problems to even hear what her team was working on. Swallowing, she nodded. "Yeah. I'm fine."

They didn't believe her. None of them believed her. And none of them tried to hide their concern. Licking her lip, she looked at her notes. "Uh. The Jupiter Heights case. Well, you all know Josh was hurt last night after someone hit him in the face with a door and stole his bag. We haven't found the bag yet, and his phone was turned off shortly after the incident, so there is no way to trace it. There were no signs that anyone broke into our condo last night. Um, Sam. Any luck finding out who the owner of the security company is?"

"TNT Security. The owner is Shane Tremant."

Eva frowned. "Of course it is. That son of a bitch has his fingers in every pot in that building."

"I hope *pot* isn't code for something." Alexa snickered, and Eva actually grinned. "Oh, look, ladies. She *does* still have a sense of humor."

Eva sighed. "I'm sorry. This case is making me crazy."

Sam nudged her again. "And here we thought it was being stuck with Joshua."

She flicked her gaze to the woman on her right. Of all the women at HEARTS, Sam was the least likely to understand. She had a carefree attitude toward life and love and everything else. She had sobered up briefly after Holly's last case had gone bad without warning, but for the most part, she'd bounced back from the incident unscathed. No. That wasn't accurate. Sam hadn't lost her carefree attitude, but she wasn't quite as unaware as she used to be. A few months ago, she really didn't understand why other members of the team took things so seriously.

Now she did. She'd learned firsthand that their cases weren't fun and games like she'd seemed to assume in the past. She was the administrator for the PIs, so she didn't spend a lot of time seeing the less appealing aspects of the job. She filed reports and monitored finances and sometimes she did deeper research, but for the most part, she was protected from the uglier side of human nature.

Realizing Holly and Jack had been in real danger had left a mark on all of them. Sam had grown up a bit, and the team had grown stronger as a unit. Before, these women had been her coworkers and friends. Now they felt more like her sisters.

"Is it being stuck with Joshua?" Tika, their primary legal investigator, pressed.

"You don't have to talk about anything private if you don't want," Holly said from across the table.

Eva did want to talk, but she didn't know where to start. She didn't want to admit how confused she was. She was a PI. She wasn't supposed to be confused and wishy-washy and so fucking mixed up inside. She wasn't supposed to be this scared.

Running her fingers through her hair, she puffed her cheeks up and blew out the breath, letting her lips vibrate as she tried to decide where to start. There was no good place, so she just opened her mouth and let the words tumble out. "I kissed him."

Sam widened her eyes. "*What?*"

Tika gasped. "When?"

"After we got home from the ER last night."

"It was the adrenaline," Rene offered. "It's normal to feel a little randy after coming down from trauma."

"No, that wasn't it." Eva frowned. "He said that he loves me." She pressed her lips together. She hadn't meant to tell them that part. She hadn't meant to ever tell anyone that part. But there it was, lingering amongst the goofy grins and quiet gasps.

The only one who hadn't reacted was Holly. If she was surprised, she didn't show it. She was a master at hiding her emotions.

"What did you say?" Tika asked with the same wonderment Eva would expect to hear from a child asking a magician how he stole her nose.

Holly cleared her throat and cast a warning glance, causing Tika to sit back. "Eva, if you'd be more comfortable with one of us staying with you, we can always make an excuse to the residents that Josh is on a business trip."

Sinking back in her chair, Eva considered the option. Without Josh there, she could probably think through whatever was happening between them. She could make sense of all the turmoil in her mind. But the thought of waking up without his arms around her caused an ache in her chest she couldn't deny. She didn't want Josh to go. She needed him there. For reasons she couldn't explain.

"Tika, Sam," Rene said as she stood. "Come with me."

Their disappointment was palpable, but Eva appreciated the thinning out of the audience. She didn't doubt for a moment that before she even got back to the condo, the rest of the team would know every word she'd said, but not having all those inquisitive eyes on her eased her stress.

Alexa moved to the chair Sam had occupied and took Eva's hand. Holly didn't move, nor did the soul-searching look in her eyes.

"I'm sorry, Eva," she said. "This is my fault. I pushed Josh on you."

Eva shook her head. "No. You were right. I've needed his help more than once."

"I knew the history there. I should have respected your request that he not move in with you."

"Holly," she stated, "this would have come to a head at some point. It's not like I can avoid him when he's basically part of the team. Besides, you were right. It is best for me to have backup since I'm actually living this case. This isn't your fault."

Alexa squeezed her hand. "I'll come stay."

Eva shook her head. "What would we say to Josh?"

"I'll handle Josh," Holly said. "Don't worry about that."

Unexpected tears sprang to Eva's eyes, and she had to swallow around the lump in her throat. "He'd never forgive me."

"I'll take the heat," Holly insisted. "In light of his

injury, I don't feel he's qualified to be on the case. There. Done."

Eva shook her head. "Don't do that, Hol. He'd be devastated. I'll be okay."

"I pushed, too," Alexa said. "I'm sorry."

Biting her lip, Eva thought back on everything that had transpired since moving into the condo at Jupiter Heights. "The thing is...you're both right. I want him there. I miss him when he's gone. But..."

"But he said the L-word and that's scary," Holly offered.

Eva had to swallow again. Even so, she could barely find her voice. "Terrifying."

"The first time Jack and I said those words, I was scared, too. It's a big step to admit you feel so deeply for someone."

"We see a lot of bad things in our line of work," Alexa said. "But we see good things, too, you know. Look at Holly and Jack."

Holly smiled. "I never would have met him if it weren't for the ugliness in the world. And he's helping me." She glanced at Alexa, tapped her fingers, and then drew a deep breath. "Listen, you know my mom was murdered when I was young."

Eva nodded slowly, not seeing what this had to do with anything.

"The thing is... Something that I have a really hard time sharing with people is that I was there, Eva. I saw it happen."

Eva's heart shattered for her friend. Suddenly so many things about Holly Austin made sense. Witnessing that kind of event at such a young age had to have left untold scars on the woman. No wonder she had a hard time showing emotion. "Hol," she whispered. "I'm so sorry."

"How long have you known me?"

"Since high school."

"And I never felt comfortable telling you that because…"

"She blames herself and thinks everyone else is going to blame her," Alexa stated.

Eva narrowed her eyes. "You knew?"

"Only because I got her drunk one night and pried it out of her." Alexa squeezed Eva's hand. "You know she likes to feel guilty about everything, even things she can't control."

Holly ignored Alexa's chastising tone. "I told Jack within a week of knowing him. I felt compelled to tell him. We have this weird connection that makes me feel…" She rolled her eyes and snorted out a half laugh. "Fuck, this sounds corny as hell. He makes me feel whole, Eva. He did from the moment we met. And I know you feel that way about Josh. You may not want to admit it, but he complements you in ways that never would have made sense until you met him. Jack needed to know this part of me in order for everything we have to fall into place. Telling him my darkest secrets, fearing he'd judge me, was one of the most terrifying things I've ever done. And I've done some crazy shit in my life."

Eva chewed at her lip before nodding. "He's so naive," she said with a laugh as she nabbed a tissue out of the box that had permanent residence on the table. "He's a coroner, for God's sake. He spends his days figuring out how people died, and he still thinks the world should be sunshine and rainbows."

"Yes, he does. He's adorable and sweet. And I believe that he does love you," Alexa offered.

Eva wiped her nose. "I think so, too." Focusing on Holly, Eva offered her a soft smile. "That cold case that you are always working on. Is that for your mom?"

Holly nodded, and in a rare show of emotion, her eyes saddened. "I've never stopped looking for the man who killed her. I never will. Jack's helping, but...the likelihood of ever finding him is fairly nonexistent."

"I'll help if you want."

Alexa brushed her hand over Eva's back. "I've been trying to get her to bring it to the meeting for months."

Eva eyed her. "You know we'd all help."

"I know. I just... When I'm ready. But we're not talking about that. We're talking about you and Josh. Do you love him?"

Biting her lip, she considered the situation for a moment before nodding. "I do, but..."

"But what?"

Wiping her eyes, she let out a long breath. "He wants me to change."

"No," Alexa said softly. "That's not what he wants, honey. He was just so scared for you. You're not the only one who has to deal with the harm people can do to each other. He sees it all the time. He didn't show it well, but he was just scared for you." Running her hand over Eva's back, she sighed. "After my sister disappeared, I couldn't leave the house. For the longest time, my *mami* wouldn't even open the blinds. *Papi* drove me to school and picked me up every day. I wasn't allowed to walk anywhere. They changed the hours of their store to accommodate my life. It was unrealistic, but they were so scared someone would kidnap me too that they lived by that fear, even if it didn't make sense. Josh knows you can't stop working as a PI. He knows that's unreasonable. But so is fear."

"My dad signed me up for jiu-jitsu after Mom was killed. Jack asked to be added to the list of people who can see my tracer," Holly said. "He wanted to see where I was all the time. I was hesitant at first. I don't want him to stalk me. But after I thought about it, I made him start carrying a tracer, too. We went through hell together, and sometimes the best way to cope isn't always logical. Sometimes I need to open that app and see his marker moving to ease my mind. And he needs to do the same. Josh works with dead people every day, Eva. It isn't hard to imagine he dreads the day someone he cares about ends up on his table."

Eva exhaled. "He has to accept I'm not altering my work to accommodate him."

"That's fair," Alexa said. "But you also have to remember that he doesn't always understand that the risk isn't the same for you as it is for most women on the street.

He knows you can take care of yourself, but sometimes knowing isn't enough to calm the worry."

Eva frowned. "I get that."

"So what are you going to do about it?" Holly asked.

Alexa smiled and nudged her. "She's going to go get her man. That's what."

Eva let out a slow breath, somehow relieved that Alexa and Holly had pushed the Josh issue. She probably never would have found the courage to make a move on her own. She'd have analyzed it forever.

"And Shane Tremant?" Holly added.

"Oh, yes," Eva stated. She might have her brain in the blender where Josh was concerned, but she knew exactly what needed to be done on the case. "I am *definitely* going to get Shane Tremant."

JOSH KNEW ALL OF EVA'S WEAKNESSES, AND SECOND only to pasta was a perfectly grilled steak. He stopped at the butcher on his way home from work. Well, their *temporary* home. They hadn't lived together when they were dating. They'd spent a lot of time at each other's homes, but they'd never moved in together. He'd felt as if they were getting close to that point—he'd been spending way more time at her apartment than his—when he'd blown it. He hadn't meant to push her too far with his worries, but his concerns were valid. What kind of jerk wouldn't be worried about his girlfriend when she dealt with criminals day in and day out?

The broken nose he'd received while helping her work a case seemed to validate the idea that he should worry about her.

But he understood now that he had worried too much and made her feel incompetent. He was doing better. He hadn't pointed out once that it could have been her who got her faced bashed in. Of course, that was mostly because she probably wouldn't have gotten her face bashed in. Eva had cobra-like reflexes. She would have stopped the door from breaking her nose and kicked the ass of the man on the other side before anyone else knew what had happened.

Instead of hovering and worrying, Josh had relished her jealousy at Courtney's come-ons and had been focused on reminding her of all the good times they'd shared while stepping back from his doubts and letting her be the strong woman he knew her to be. Even though he was terrified that she'd get herself into some kind of mess she couldn't escape, having his own ass kicked had somehow made him see she was right all along—he was a much bigger target for violence than she was.

He'd slept well the night before. Sure, that could be attributed to the impact the chemical breakdown of the drugs he'd been given at the ER had on his ventrolateral preoptic nucleus, but also because he finally got it. The distortion he'd had on reality had finally cleared. Eva was tougher than he'd ever be. That didn't mean he wouldn't worry about her, but being on the receiving end of getting his butt handed to him by a locker room door gave him the perspective to really appreciate her strength.

He wet his fingers and flicked them toward the grill top he was preheating, but the water didn't sizzle when it landed. The grill wasn't ready, which was fine. He had a few more seasonings to add to his homemade steak rub before searing in the flavors. Looking over the options that sat on the two-tiered lazy Susan tucked in the corner, he started to reach for garlic salt but faltered in his movements. Granted, the kitchen had been fully stocked when they'd moved in, and he couldn't possibly have memorized everything, but he was certain there had not been a bottle of sunflower oil tucked next to the olive and vegetable oils.

He stared at the label, trying to jar his memory, before he grabbed the seasonings he'd intended. Sprinkling additional flavor onto the raw steaks, he brushed his hands on his apron and tested the head on the grill again. His flicking was met with the telltale sizzle of a preheated grill.

"Perfect," he muttered to himself. He dropped two sirloins onto the surface and then washed his hands and headed into the bedroom. Eva would chop his fingers off if she caught him touching her equipment, but he wasn't about to text her and have her think he was an idiot if the oil had been there all along. Turning on her camera, he scrolled through the photos she'd taken the last time they'd returned to the condo.

She did that each time and compared them to the last.

Each time, she made notes and told him he'd be the first to know if she found anything. He took that to mean she hadn't. But maybe he had. Flipping through the images, he stopped on the last series of close-ups on the kitchen. He swallowed hard as he confirmed what he was certain he already knew—that bottle of oil had not been there yesterday.

And they hadn't gone grocery shopping since then. That bottle did not belong in their kitchen.

He turned off the camera and sank onto the edge of the bed. What should he do? What would Eva do? He spied the thermal camera in her bag of tricks and picked it up. Clutching the camera, he looked through the bedroom door toward the kitchen. If there were a camera in that bottle, the heat would show up as a white blotch in the thermal image. He knew that much from his mini detection training session with Alexa.

He should confirm his suspicions before taking them to Eva. Then she wouldn't have to know if he were wrong. He could act like this never happened. But if he was right, he could prove to her that he wasn't as much of a pain in her backside as she thought. Turning the camera on as he went back to the kitchen, he scanned the bottle and his breath caught. The center of the label had a distinct white aura that definitely wouldn't be there if the bottle only contained oil.

Holy cow.

Holy. Freaking. Cow.

He was being recorded. Someone had broken into

their condo and placed a camera, and he was being recorded. Setting the camera down, he pulled his phone from his pocket and fumbled to get the text app open. Finding Eva's name, he fervently typed: *Where are you?*

HEARTS, she answered.

Get home. Think there's a camera here.

Do NOT touch anything! On the way.

He sank onto the barstool, not moving until the scent of cooking beef reminded him the steaks were overdue for flipping. He scowled at a sudden realization. If Eva was at the office, she wouldn't be alone. And she likely wouldn't arrive at the condo alone.

Grabbing his phone again, he typed: *How many for dinner?*

5.

Six. Because he doubted she counted him in that.

Including you, she added.

Huh. How about that? Drumming his fingertips on the counter, he tried to figure the best way to change his dinner plan to cover five. Egg noodles and gravy would take his intended steak-and-steamed-veggies dinner for two to somewhat decent serving sizes for five. He didn't have rolls, but he did have a loaf of artisan bread and real butter. That would have to do. Getting to work, hyper-aware of the camera watching him, he started water boiling for the noodles and whipped up a big batch of brown gravy.

Not his best work, but by the time Eva, Rene, Alexa, and Holly rushed in, he was almost ready to serve.

"Dinner first," he said before Eva could ask about the camera.

She opened her mouth, but the other women headed right to the table. "Traitors," she muttered.

"We're hungry," Rene said, reminding Josh the woman had what sometimes seemed like supernaturally strong hearing.

He smiled but then winced a bit. He kept forgetting how tender his damned black eyes were.

Eva tilted her head, and what could pass for sympathy touched her eyes. "You look like a bad lightweight boxer, Joshie."

He chuckled.

Holding up her fists in a fighting posture, she smirked. "Maybe I should show you a few moves, hmm?"

"Or buy me a football helmet."

She pretended to ponder his suggestion before changing the subject. "Where is it?"

"Dinner first."

Cocking a brow, she pressed, "I can find it myself."

"I know. But I went to the trouble of cooking dinner. You're going to eat while it's hot." He hefted the pot of noodles, gravy, and chopped steaks. "Grab the pitcher of iced tea I made earlier."

"Well, someone is wearing his bossy pants this evening," she whispered but did as he told her.

He winked and carried the dish to the table. After serving the women, including Eva, Josh sat next to her and watched his friends dig into the last-minute dinner he'd made. Funny how something so simple made him feel so complete. He'd been an only child growing up and had always struggled to find his place in the world, but he'd certainly found it now.

"How's your face, Josh?" Holly asked as she grabbed a chunk of sliced bread.

"Painful. I'm going to try really hard to never have a broken nose again."

Rene shook her head. "Your life is bound to be filled with disappointment if you set such high goals."

He chuckled and then winced. "Don't make me laugh. Seriously. That hurts."

"Sorry."

But Rene didn't look sorry. And he wasn't sorry, either. As much as he knew this group had accepted him, he had never felt as much a part of HEARTS as he did after earning his own war wounds. Now when they sat around talking about scars and injuries, as they tended to do when sharing drinks at their favorite pub, he could add something like "remember when I got my nose broken on that voyeur case..." instead of his usual scientific explanations for how those injuries happened or healed that they graciously tolerated but were clearly uninterested in.

Eva had barely taken the last bite of her noodles before sitting back. "All right. Dinner's over. Where's the goods?"

Josh smiled at her, not quite as wide as before since his face hurt like hell. He liked having the power over her for once. Usually she had a leg up on him. He quite enjoyed being the one in control. He sat back, as she had done, only he crossed his arms and gave her as smug of a look as he could manage. "How about dessert? We have half a gallon of praline pecan ice cream. Anyone?"

"*Joshua*," Eva chastised.

He loved the feisty tone of her voice. "In the sunflower oil."

She playfully narrowed her ice-blue eyes at him before pushing herself up. The teasing smile on his face faltered when he noticed the other women looking at him. Holly stared, barely showing emotion as always. Alexa had her brows raised and a knowing smirk on her lips. Rene's eyes were a warning. She had to know Josh would never do anything to hurt Eva, but that would never stop her from being protective of her teammate and friend. Josh respected that.

As Holly cleared the table, Alexa spread a towel on the surface and Rene dug into her bag. Josh sat back, watching the women work in perfect unison. By the time Eva put on her latex gloves and carried the sunflower oil to the table, they were ready to check the bottle for fingerprints. Rene dusted, her frown deepening with each stroke of her brush and latent powder.

"This is clean," she finally declared.

"But the SD card isn't," Eva said. She twisted the bottle. It separated in the middle, and she was able to pull out the small camera. As she'd done before, she used tweezers to carefully pull the card out and put it in her laptop after bringing it to life.

She rubbed her hands together. "All right, ladies—"

"And gentleman," Josh added.

"Let's catch us a pervert."

Eva clicked to start the video playing. The image was all black. Still black. And...black some more. Then grays and whites started to come into view. A hand moved from in front of the lens and revealed...a black mask, black hoodie, and black jeans.

"What the fuck?" Eva spat.

"Smart little criminal," Holly muttered.

Disappointment fell over Eva's face. Josh rubbed his palm up and down her back but then dropped his hand after catching Alexa grinning at him. Returning his attention to the screen, he narrowed his eyes as the criminal adjusted the bottle. "Hey. That's not Shane Tremant. It can't be."

"How can you tell?" Holly asked.

"Because when he caught me with his fob, I remember thinking his hands were big enough to crush my skull without much effort. Those are not Shane's giant head-crushing hands."

Eva leaned closer, peering as if she could see through the mask if she just tried hard enough. "Holy shit."

"What?" Rene demanded.

Eva paused the video and backed it up a few frames. "Look at that."

Rene also leaned in and squinted her dark eyes. "*What?*"

Josh widened his eyes. "Boobs," he blurted out.

Holly flicked the back of his head, but Eva tapped the screen.

"Boobs," she agreed. "Our pervert has boobs. See the bulge in the hoodie right there. *He's* a *she*." Eva let out a half laugh as she leaned back. "Wow. I did *not* see that coming."

12

Eva couldn't wrap her head around what she'd seen. The voyeur was a woman. Not to sound like Josh, but statistically speaking, that simply didn't make sense. Voyeurs tended to be middle-aged married males. Shane Tremants and Neal Prices. A woman? Damn. Eva had to rethink everything she'd put together for this case.

The other HEARTS had barely walked out the door before she'd spread her notes over the table to scour every bit of evidence she'd gathered. What had she missed? And how the hell had she missed it?

Staring at the bedroom ceiling, she rolled the case over in her mind for the hundredth time since crawling into bed next to Josh. She had no choice, really—even if the latest bit of information hadn't been eating at her gut, she couldn't possibly sleep while lying this close to Josh after realizing how deeply she felt for him. If she weren't obsessing about the case, she'd likely have climbed on top of him by now.

Something that was still far too tempting.

Slipping from beneath the blankets, she headed to the dining room table, where she still had papers spread everywhere, easing the bedroom door closed behind her. Wincing as she flipped on the overhead light, she filled a glass with water and stood over the table.

"Okay," she whispered to the papers. "What did you miss?"

Neal and Shane were clearly working on something together. Shane's wife Tiffany was sleeping with Courtney. Courtney didn't seem to like Neal or Shane...which made sense if she was sleeping with his wife. And she was hitting on Josh so blatantly. Why?

"Oh. Oh!" As she thought of Courtney's reactions anytime someone mentioned being in a relationship, two pieces of the puzzle clicked into place.

"Eva," Josh said with a sleep-thickened voice, "save it for tomorrow."

Glancing up, she caught her breath. Because getting a T-shirt on and off was risky business with his broken nose, he'd opted to sleep in nothing but shorts that hung low on his slender hips. Eva let her gaze sweep over the pale skin covering the muscles that were enough to be seen but not bulging like some kind of gym rat. She'd never considered how sexy it was that Joshua spent more time nurturing his mind than obsessing about building muscles. But it was sexy. It was...*Josh*. And Josh was sexy as hell in her mind.

Clearing her throat, Eva gestured toward her notes. "Twice now I've seen Courtney react to comments about people in relationships. I didn't get it before, but after seeing her and Tiffany together in that video, I think she wants more than just a secret rendezvous here or there. She wants a serious relationship, but Tiffany is married to Shane. Not necessarily *happily* married and obviously not committed to him, but she is definitely committed to his wallet. She's not going to leave him, and Courtney has to know that." She bit her lip and looked at her notebook again. "But what does that have to do with the voyeur? That's what I can't work out."

Nibbling at her thumbnail, she dug deeper into her mind. "You said it sounded like Neal and Shane were whispering about me knowing something?"

"They said *she*. I assumed it was you. Could have been someone else."

She snapped her fingers as she lifted her gaze to his. "What if *she* is Brenda Price? What if Tiffany isn't the only bisexual Tremant? Two things are very clear: Neal and Shane are in cahoots over something, and Brenda is intensely angry about something. Maybe Neal and Shane are sleeping together, too, and Brenda figured it out." Her excitement faded a bit. "But that doesn't explain why she was so hostile toward me or her warning that I'm *their* type." Raking her fingers through her hair, she exhaled in a show of how deep her frustration ran. "Damn it. Why isn't this coming together?"

"Because it is after two o'clock in the morning."

Dropping her hands, she offered him a slight smile. "I know. I couldn't sleep. Sorry if I woke you. I was trying to be quiet."

"You were quiet. I felt you get out of bed." Crossing the room, he moved behind her as if he were going to look at her notes, too.

His spicy scent surrounded her moments before he put his hands on her shoulders and his heat warmed her back. He rubbed his thumbs into her shoulders, working on the knots that always seemed to gather there. Her breath caught at the feel of him touching her. Her train of thought didn't simply fall off the tracks; her concentration nosedived off a bridge and hit several ledges before crashing into a rocky bottom, exploding on impact.

"You need to rest, baby girl."

Baby girl? She smiled at the term that he'd started using the day their relationship changed from friends to more but hadn't used since once she'd ended things between them months ago. She'd always cringed inside, hating how his words highlighted his lack of faith in her. This time, however, her heart swelled so much, she thought it might burst from her chest and sing a show tune right there on the table.

"I can't rest," she said on a sigh. "Not when I have to start over."

Lowering his hands, he wrapped his arms around her waist and pulled her against him. "You aren't starting over. You have quite a bit to go on, actually. It's just that there are a lot of new suspects to look at since most of the residents are women," he said.

Eva blinked long and slow. She heard his words, but they didn't make sense. "Hmm?"

"The woman who placed the camera is likely a resident, right?"

Oh. The case. Right. "Yeah. To get access to the condos, she probably lives here." Her words were muttered, mostly because her mind was consumed by the heat that was burning into her skin through her thin shirt. She'd barely been able to clear her head since getting home. Closing her eyes, she replayed the conversation she'd had with Alexa and Holly earlier. She'd admitted to them—and to herself—that she loved Josh. Ever since then, the rabid elephant in the room seemed to have ripped her heart open and exposed the gaping wound to the brutal emotions that love brought with it.

Josh had already hurt her once. And here she was, tempted to ask him to do it again. She thought he'd learned his lesson. She *hoped* he'd learned his lesson. And she hoped that she'd learned some things, too. Like how to not always expect the worst from people. How to not always anticipate the worst.

And how to forgive his missteps and let them go so they could move forward.

None of those things came easy to Eva, but she finally understood she had to figure that out if she and Josh were going to really get the second chance they both seemed to want.

"This really has you shaken," Josh said, squeezing her, seemingly unaware of the torture he was inflicting with his close proximity.

Sinking her teeth into her bottom lip, Eva revisited her earlier assessment.

She loved Josh. She couldn't imagine her life without him. Thanks to Courtney's blatant flirting, Eva now had an inkling of what it would feel like for him to be with someone else. She found the idea unbearable. Seeing him hurt, watching the doctor set his nose and knowing he was in pain, had felt like a knife twisting in her gut. She never wanted to see him hurt again or feel the fear that she could lose him.

"Hey," he said, turning her to face him. "Are you okay?"

"No," she confessed on a whisper. "I'm not. I'm so far from being okay that I don't know what I'm supposed to do."

He stared at her with obvious concern. "Baby, what's wrong?"

"This." She gestured between them. "This thing between us. It isn't going to go away, is it?"

His silence felt like a million punches to her gut. She couldn't breathe while he seemed to debate his answer. "No," he said after what had to have been hours. Maybe days. "It isn't going to go away. We're connected somehow, and...and that isn't going away."

She swallowed hard. Hearing him confirm what she'd

already accepted terrified her. "I know I didn't show it well, but I was so scared when you got hurt."

"I know you were." He brushed his hands over her arms. "If it's any consolation," he said with a slight grin, "so was I."

She laughed for a moment before letting her smile fade. Nodding toward the table, she said, "This is what I do, Josh. This is who I am. I can't change that. I don't *want* to change that."

"I don't want you to."

"But you do. How many times did you say—"

"I was wrong, Eva." Taking her hands, he stared at them as his shoulders sagged. "I was worried about you, and *I* didn't show *that* well." Meeting her gaze again, he said, "We both have some work to do, but I would never want you to change. You're right, this is who you are. This is who I fell madly in love with."

His words were like an unexpected splash of ice water washing over her on a hot day. She gasped involuntarily, but the ensuing relief was profound. Her heart dared to acknowledge a spark of hope. Resting her palms to his cheeks, careful of his blackened eyes and broken nose, she whispered, "I don't want you to change, either. I love your nerdy self." She grinned as he pulled her closer to him.

"Will you hurt me if I kiss you?"

Getting onto her tiptoes so she could slide her arms around his neck, she whispered back, "I'll hurt you if you don't."

He smashed his mouth to hers, possessing her in a way

that was usually saved for her. Josh had never been the assertive one. She didn't remind him of that. She dug her fingers in his hair and opened her mouth to his demanding tongue. He gripped her thighs just under her ass and lifted her onto the table. She leaned back when he broke the kiss and hissed under his breath.

"Joshie," she breathed.

"I'm okay." He dove back in, kissing her hard again.

This time, Eva pulled his hair until he put a few inches between them. "Stop."

"I'm sorry. I thought—"

She clung to him so he couldn't step away. Wrapping her legs around him, she secured his body against hers, sighing at the feel of his erection pressing against her thin shorts. She kissed him lightly then, sweetly, like he always kissed her. "We can do this without causing further injury to your face." Running her hand down his chest, she slipped it beneath the elastic band of his pants and cupped his ass. The feel of his muscles rippling under her palm sent a thrill through her. Pulling his body to hers, she ground her sex against his. "This is all I want. You and me. Like this again."

Resting his forehead to hers, he exhaled slowly. "So do I. More than you know." His next kiss was sweet, soft... pure Josh, and she nearly melted against him. "I'll do better this time. I promise."

She was tempted to tease him, to make a sex joke to avoid the seriousness of his words. The sarcasm wouldn't surface. Instead, she kissed him with all the tenderness she'd denied him for too long. Stroking her fingers through his hair, she smiled. "Me, too."

"I meant what I said, Eva. I love you."

"I love you, too."

He lifted her off the table, his hands gripping her thighs, and carried her to the bedroom. The light coming from the doorway was just enough to appreciate the sweet way he looked her body over as he eased her onto the pile of crumpled blankets. He kneeled before her, tugging her shorts over her hips and down her legs. As he eased her pants over her ankles, she arched up enough to pull her shirt off and toss it aside.

God, how she'd missed this—his kisses gliding up her legs, adding fuel to her fire with every inch he covered. His hands, soft and gentle, brushing over her skin in a ritual that had always made her feel cherished. Before, she hadn't appreciated the slow burn he had a way of creating. She'd just wanted him in her, quenching her internal thirst for him. However, as he nipped at that spot just behind her knee, she bit her lip and let the sensation fill her.

His teeth scraping across her flesh sent ripples of heat to her core, making her body want to scream for his. Instead of pulling him up, demanding he satisfy her immediately as she'd always done, she let him torment her in the best possible way—with his lips, tongue, and teeth. They put her under some kind of sexual spell that she never wanted to break. So lost in the feel of him that she actually gasped, startled, at the feel of his thumb rubbing over her center. He massaged, nipped, and kissed until she screamed out.

"Josh," she panted, "you're killing me."

"I know."

Shit. She hadn't realized how close his mouth was to her core until his breath heated the skin he'd manipulated with his hand. Fingers slid into her opening as his tongue flicked her clitoris. Grabbing fistfuls of blanket, she reminded herself not to buck into him. The man was injured enough, but damned if she didn't want to shove his face harder between her legs. Forcing herself to restrain her movements was taking too much of her focus. "Come here," she ordered, reaching for him.

He licked at her several times, thrusting his fingers in time with his mouth, before whispering, "You have no idea how much I've missed tasting you."

She let a sultry laugh rip from her throat. "Not nearly as much as I've missed being tasted."

Sliding up her body, taking a moment to give her nipples the same treatment he'd given her clit, he kissed her. His fingers never stopped their skillful movements, but as he bit her bottom lip, his thumb joined them, and her body lurched. She called his name as he sent her soaring and then falling into an abyss she hoped there was no end to.

JOSH COULDN'T TAKE ANOTHER MOMENT OF HIS

sweet torture. As much as Eva was going insane, he was even further gone. He had to have her. When they were dating, they'd relied on her birth control pill for protection, but they hadn't been dating for a few months. He wasn't sure where they stood on such things now. "I don't have any protection," he said.

She fell flat against the bed. The light was dim, but he saw something like hurt in her eyes. "Do I need to worry about where you've been?"

"No. I just...didn't want to assume we were still okay with that."

"We're still okay," she whispered as she gripped his hips.

Pulling him forward, she rolled her head back, and he groaned as her heat enveloped him. With their bodies connected in the most intimate way as he dug his fingers into her hair and kissed her lips while she wrapped her legs around his, Josh's soul nearly cried out with the peace that washed over him. He was home. His body, mind, and spirit were finally back where he belonged.

Moving with her, feeling her returning every ounce of love he was offering, he thought he was going to lose control. Damn it, he wasn't ready for this to end yet. As always, Eva seemed to be in tune with him. She unraveled her legs and pushed him onto his back. Taking several deep breaths, he silently thanked her for the reprieve he wouldn't have given himself. He was far too weak to deny himself of her.

Catching his breath, he soaked in the feel of her hands

on his chest, her kisses along his jaw. He'd just caught his breath when she leaned over him and, much like he'd done to her, sank her teeth into his bottom lip.

"Ready?" she asked on a breath.

He laughed quietly. "Ready."

Rotating her hips, she slid him back into her body, leaned back, and put her hands to his thighs. This was his favorite. As much as he loved covering her with his body as if he were dominating every inch of her, this—Eva straddling him, bending in a way to increase the friction of their connected bodies—was his favorite.

Gripping her hips, holding her steady, he ground his heels into the mattress so he could meet every rotation of her hips with a thrust of his. Within seconds they found the rhythm they both had come to know so well. *Grind-thrust. Grind-thrust.* Her fingernails dug into his thighs as his fingertips pressed into her hips. He knew her tells as much as he knew his own. The moment she started panting his name, he cupped her breasts, squeezing until her body spasmed around him. He shoved into her, hard, pinching her nipples between his fingers until she cried out.

Feeling her orgasm sent him spiraling into his own. One more firm thrust, and he started pulsating into her. She collapsed onto him, resting her head on his shoulder as he hugged her close to him, both breathless and sweaty.

Stroking her hair, he gulped several deep breaths before placing a string of kisses along her shoulder. "I'll fill the tub."

"It's almost three in the morning."

"I don't care. We've missed so much. We need to catch up."

"You'll be exhausted at work tomorrow."

He kissed her again. "I think I need a sick day to recover from my injury."

She laughed as she fell onto him. "I think you need a sick day to make up for lost time with your girlfriend."

He hugged her closer at the title she'd given herself. *Girlfriend* wasn't enough, would never been a strong enough word to describe what she was to him. But it would do.

For tonight.

Rolling her onto her back, he stroked her hair from her face. "Give me just a minute to get the water started and then join me." A quick kiss and he pushed himself up and into the bathroom. By the time she joined him, he was able to help her in to sink into bellybutton-deep water. The tub needed a few more inches of hot water before the jets could be turned on, but that didn't stop Josh from sliding in with her.

He grabbed a washcloth and her lavender-scented body wash to get started on the ceremony he'd been dreaming about since they'd moved into the condo. Sex with Eva was incredible. The bonding that took place afterward was even better. Though they'd bathed together the other night, though she'd let him touch her and wash her and use her touch to soothe his soul, it hadn't been complete. The ritual had been missing a vital element. The intimacy that had so tightly held them together.

She leaned back, closed her eyes, and moaned softly as he started rubbing the rag over her skin. He'd get his turn sooner or later, but he took his time to enjoy this. Smiling when she rolled her head and lifted her heavy lids to look at him.

"This is the best," she said.

"Yes, it is." He kissed the wet arch of her foot before lowering her leg into the steadily rising water. He was working on her other calf when she sat up enough to press the button to start the jets.

"You know, if you do stay home tomorrow, you can help me set up surveillance."

He smiled, excited at the idea of helping her case again. She hadn't been open to the idea since he'd taken a door to the face. She'd specifically told him to stay out of the way before he got hurt worse. With the tub nearly full, he turned off the water. The jets were loud enough, but without the water running, they could hear each other a better. "What's your plan?"

"Well, since it's illegal to hack the existing cameras and Shane Tremant's company doesn't provide more than an hour of memory, I plan on hiding my own cameras. In the hallways," she clarified before he could ask. "I should be able to catch the she-perv coming and going out of the condos."

"When will you question Shane about the lax security?"

"Tomorrow if possible. But I also need to clarify some things with Neal Price."

"I want you to..." He caught himself before telling her to be safe.

A slow smile spread across her face. "Yes, Joshie. I'll be careful."

"I know you will." Digging his fingertips into her calf, he worked over the muscle. "I trust you to take care of yourself, Eva. But I'd be a jerk not to worry."

Holding his gaze, she conceded his point with one nod. "Yes, you would be."

Tugging her foot as he scooted forward, Josh settled between her knees as she spread her legs and sat to meet him. She draped her arms over his shoulders and stared into his eyes. She'd wrapped an elastic band around the pile of hair, but a strand had fallen free, and he tucked it behind her ear. "I meant what I said. I'm going to do better at showing you that I believe in you. Because I do. You are amazing at what you do. If I hadn't known it before, which I did, I wouldn't be able to deny it after spending the last few days watching you sort out this mess. You're brilliant." Running his hands over her back, he kissed the top of her nose. "I'm honored to call you mine."

A cocky grin touched her lips. "Does that make you mine?"

"Unequivocally."

She put her lips to his in a kiss, as if it were a claim to mark what was hers. "Courtney will be so disappointed."

He grinned. "Something tells me that isn't new to her. Sleeping with a married woman never ends well."

"You know from experience?"

"Several of my patients do."

She rolled her head back and laughed, giving him perfect access to kiss her neck. He did. Never mind that the angle put a bit of pressure on his upper jaw and sent painful ripples through the rest of his tender face. Her laugh ended with a sigh as she fisted strands of his hair.

"Don't tempt me." Her voice held a sultry tone. "It's been too long since we've been like this."

"I know." He licked over her flesh. "That's exactly why I'm tempting you."

Reaching between them, she stroked him back to a full erection before shifting her hips and easing him into her. Again, they fell into a pattern they knew so well, moving together as the hot water surrounded them and the jets added to the sensual feelings.

When they moved in together—yes, *when*—they'd have to move into Eva's apartment. His bathtub was not nearly large enough to accommodate bath sex.

13

Eva touched the gun hidden under her suit jacket, confirmation that her protection was there if needed. Not that she thought she would, but she was about to call Neal Price out on some of his bullshit, and those conversations held a higher risk of going south than most. Pounding her fist on his unit door, she took a step back. Her posture wasn't defensive but ready. Her nerves had been on edge since leaving her condo.

In one sense, she was so much closer to catching her suspect, but in another sense, she was back at square one. Now that she knew Neal Price hadn't placed the cameras, she could get a bit tougher with him. His behavior from the moment he'd hired her had been off. She was about to demand he tell her why.

The door opened, and Cody stuck her head out. "What do you want?"

"Is your dad home?"

"No."

A cobra likely had a better personality than Cody. Was probably sweeter, too. What was up with this kid? "Know where he is?"

"No."

"Know when he'll be back?"

"No."

Putting her hand up, Eva stopped Cody from closing the door on her. Staring the surly teen down, she forced as nice a smile as she could manage. "Is he at work?"

"Why don't you check?"

"Cody?" a male voice called. Neal pulled the door open wider and frowned at Eva.

She smirked at Cody, who rolled her eyes and stormed off. "Morning."

"I thought I told you to stay away from my family."

"I'm not here to see your family. I'm here to see you."

"I'll be back," he called into his condo.

"Whatever," his daughter replied.

Stepping into the hallway, he pulled the door shut. "What?"

"You're awfully hostile considering you hired me," she said quietly. "Why is that?"

"I don't like your approach."

"What approach is that?"

He moved around her, toward the elevator. Pressing the button with his thumb, he ground his teeth so tightly the muscles in his jaw bulged. "How much longer is this going to take?" he asked once they were inside the car.

"I guess that depends."

"On what?"

"On a few things."

The door slid open, and she gestured for him to go first. He had an air of hostility about him, and she didn't want him behind her. If he decided to make a stupid move, she wanted to see him coming. "Let's sit there." She gestured toward two chairs in the lobby.

"I'd prefer to do this in private."

"I wouldn't."

They stared at each other for a few moments before he crossed the open lobby and sat in one of the chairs she'd suggested.

"What's going on?" he demanded.

Sitting across from him, she held his gaze, unwavering. "I know Shane Tremant owns the security company you hired for the building. The one that is providing minimal storage, despite you knowing there are crimes being committed."

His jaw muscles flexed again. "I told you I'd handle that."

"Your records indicate HOA paid for top-of-the-line security, yet that's not what Jupiter Heights is receiving."

"I'll take care of it, Ms. Thompson."

She didn't flinch at his firm tone. "Where is the HOA's money going, Mr. Price?"

"The security package—"

"The security package they are paying for is not what they are receiving. *Where* is the money going?"

"I didn't hire you to look into the HOA finances."

"You mean you didn't hire me to catch you embezzling from the HOA."

Price jumped to his feet. So did Eva. She might be nearly a foot shorter than him, but she wasn't intimidated and wanted to make certain he knew it. She held her left hand up, a subtle warning for him to stay back while her right hand opened her coat enough to show her weapon.

He snorted. "You going to shoot me?"

"You going to make me? Sit down."

Easing back into the chair, he blew out a slow breath. "We needed the money for a start-up."

"We?"

"*I.*"

She smirked. "Nah. Too late for that. Shane is obviously in on this. What about Brenda? Is that why she's so angry?"

A bitter laugh left him. "Are you kidding me? She doesn't care how I pay for her manicures and dye jobs, as long as I do."

"Sounds like she and Tiffany have more than a few things in common."

He narrowed his eyes at her. "I didn't hire you to look into my wife's affair either, Ms. Thompson."

Eva resisted the urge to blink in surprise. He hadn't said *affairs,* as in her to-do list or her comings and goings. He'd said *affair*, as in extramarital sexual relations. In response to her comment about his wife and Tiffany?

Wow. Brenda Price was right; Mrs. Tremant certainly did get around.

Frowning, Neal sat back. "Yeah. I know about that. How did you figure it out?"

She hadn't, but she wasn't going to confess that. "That's what I do, Mr. Price."

He scoffed. "You have any idea how many times Shane and I paid for them to take weekends way? Resorts, concerts, girls' nights out. I don't even know how long they had us snowed before I walked in on them. In my own fucking bedroom. Brenda says they *accidently* slept together after getting drunk while the four of us were on vacation in the Caribbean. Shane and I went diving. Apparently so did our wives."

"Are they still sleeping together?"

"No. I gave them an ultimatum. Knock it off or leave. I'm pretty sure Brenda was ready to walk out the door, but no way Tiffany was going to end the free ride she'd landed by marrying Shane."

"You said *you* gave them the ultimatum. Where did Shane stand on their affair?"

Running his hand over his thinning hair, Neal scoffed. "Shane's a good guy."

Eva thought that was debatable. She'd just confirmed they were thieves. She opted not to point that out.

"But he's a guy's guy, if you know what I mean. The only thing he wanted was for them to let him join in the fun. He thought I was crazy because I didn't want to share my wife. He even took me out one night to have a couple of beers to try to talk me into it. 'Tiffany says she and Brenda are cool with it,' he said. 'We'd be living like porn stars.'" Neal let a little laugh leave him. "That's all good in a fantasy, but...I didn't want to watch him or Tiffany screwing my wife, and I didn't want her coming home to me knowing she'd been somewhere else. I put my foot down. I told her if I found out she was still screwing around on me, I'd kick her ass out. Let Shane and Tiffany support her. And good luck explaining that to Cody."

"I'm sorry," Eva said sincerely. The deep frown and sorrow in his eyes revealed how painful this had been. Neal was obviously torn up about his wife's infidelity.

"I watch her like a hawk. One misstep, just one, and I'll wash my hands of her. Cody is sixteen. She can cope with her parents splitting. Brenda knows it, too. She's mad as hell, but I don't care. She's the cheater. She doesn't get a pass."

"Mr. Price, does Shane know about the hidden camera found in Wendi Carter's condo?"

"No."

"Does he know who I am?"

He shook his head.

"When I spoke with Brenda the other day, she warned me that I was just *their* type. What did she mean by that?"

He lowered his gaze and stared at his hands.

"Is there a reason most of the residents in this building are fair-haired females like me?"

Leaning back, he looked around the lobby. "Shane and Tiffany... Not having Brenda and me in the mix didn't stop them from having their fun. Finding out what Tiffany had been up to, and was willing to get up to, was like setting a fire inside that man's head. He has a type. Just look at his wife. After I shit-canned the idea of having a quad with them, they decided to find someone else. Tiffany didn't need or want another man, just another woman...or women. Shane couldn't have been happier about that. In his mind, the more the merrier. Every time a condo comes open, Shane pushes me to bring in..."

"Sexual prey for him and his wife?"

He had the sense to look ashamed of himself.

"And what do you get in return?"

His sense of disgrace obviously ran deep. Eva liked that. She didn't feel bad for him, but she did appreciate he at least had the morality to know he'd done something to be embarrassed about. Even if he didn't have enough to stop this violation of his neighbors before it started.

"I needed money to start a new company. I said that."

"Shane worked his magic to get you on as HOA president so you could work together to embezzle money, and you pay him back by approving purchase offers from women he's attracted to."

He nodded. "Yeah. That about sums it up."

"*About*? Did I miss something?"

He looked around the lobby again.

Resting her elbows on her knees, she closed some of the distance between them. "Neal, whatever you're holding back, I *will* figure it out on my own. Right now, I'm still working this case for you, but if you continue to lie and deceive me, when I find out what other secrets you're keeping, I might not be on your side any longer. Trust me when I tell you that you want me on your side."

Silence fell thick between them before he decided to speak. "I lied."

"About?"

"About needing the money for a startup. There is no business."

Eva considered what other reasons he would have to be dumping money into Shane's security company. "He's blackmailing you?"

"He doesn't see it that way. He asked the board to go with his company, and they were happy to. They wanted to support their neighbor's endeavor, you know. I didn't realize he was cheating us until Wendi Carter found that camera. I asked him to check the surveillance, and he danced around until he had to admit that there wasn't any. I was pissed. I told him to fix it or I was going to cancel the contract. That's when he let me know Tiffany has video of her and Brenda together. He threatened to share it with anyone who would watch it. The prick. I hired you hoping you'd catch him putting cameras in the condos. Then I'd be rid of him, could cancel the contract with his company, and not have him threatening my wife anymore." Lifting his gaze to her, he let out a breath that didn't seem to ease much of his frustration. "I know it's him, I just can't prove it."

"It's not him."

"The fuck it isn't."

"Mr. Price, someone hid a camera in my kitchen. The suspect wore a mask so we couldn't see *her* face, but it was, without a doubt, a woman."

His face paled, but then his eyes lit as if he'd solved a great mystery. "Tiffany."

"Possibly. Why would she put a camera in my condo?"

"Because Shane is frothing at the mouth to get you into bed. Has been since he saw you working out. He asked to see the resident file for you and Josh."

"Did you show it to him?"

He nodded. "We faked your purchase, so I don't think he could get much off of it."

"Wrong. He got plenty off that report. Including the pattern Josh and I have for leaving for work and coming home. He knew exactly when our condo would be empty so Tiffany, if that's who it was, could plant a camera. Why are they planting cameras in condos? The camera was in the kitchen. If they were trying to get something smutty, why not put it in the bedroom?"

He looked at her as if she were too dumb to exist. "If he wants you, and Tiffany agrees, they'll stop at nothing to get you. Has Tiffany thrown herself at you yet?"

"Not exactly, but I have to say I did feel a bit like I was being groomed when I went shopping with her."

"What about your boyfriend? Has she come on to him yet?"

She sat back, thinking about the odd evening she and Josh had spent with Courtney...the woman whom they'd also seen on video sleeping with Tiffany Tremant.

"I guess she has." He smirked. "If they don't think you're open to sleeping with them, don't doubt for a minute they won't sink so low as to get evidence of your boyfriend cheating on you. Once you're brokenhearted, Tiffany will become your best friend."

"And more," Eva said thoughtfully.

"Only if you let her."

"Did they show interest in Wendi Carter before she discovered the camera?"

"Shane did. Wendi's boyfriend threatened to kick his ass, and then Tiffany cornered Wendi. It was ugly."

"So their advances fell flat with Wendi and they turned on her."

"I don't know their motive, but if I had to guess, they probably wanted to make her life a living hell so she'd sell and move out. Everyone here knows these units don't stay empty long. If someone wants to sell, they won't have any issue finding a buyer."

"Do you really believe they'd go to such lengths to get rid of one person who wasn't interested in having sexual relations with them?"

"I don't know. This entire situation is crazy."

"Well, that we can agree upon. What happened to the camera from Wendi's apartment?"

Neal frowned. "I don't know. It really did go missing from my desk. Listen, if it isn't Shane, then it has to be Tiffany. I don't know who else would do this."

Tiffany Tremant definitely could have been the slim figure on the video camera. And Shane would know enough about security cameras to tell her to cover her face so the footage didn't give her away. That also meant he probably knew enough to cover his tracks when buying the cameras, which would explain why Sam still hadn't been able to trace the purchase.

"Is there anything else you've been keeping from me, Mr. Price?"

"I didn't know what I was getting into. I was trying to protect my wife. I didn't know Shane and Tiffany would..."

"Manipulate women for sex?"

"Yeah. That."

She didn't approve of the choices he'd made, but she did believe the situation had gotten out of his control before he understood the real consequences of his actions. "You're going to do two things by the end of the week, Mr. Price. First, you're going to refund the HOA, and second, you're going to have real security installed by someone other than Shane Tremant."

He opened his mouth, clearly to argue, but then he nodded.

"I want to see proof those things are done. Or I will notify the police of your participation, willing or not, in what's been going on here."

"It'll get done," he muttered.

Standing upright, she looked down her nose at him. "You may not have intended to, but your attempt to cover for your wife has put every woman in this building in a position to be violated in more ways than I can explain. Do you understand that?"

"Yes."

"Wendi Carter is suffering tremendously after realizing she'd been watched. Imagine how she would feel if she'd been unknowingly manipulated into a sexual relationship with a married couple."

"I get it, Ms. Thompson."

She shook her head at him. "I don't think you do. But you will, if any of the women they've corralled into their little sex ring has been forced, in any way, to do something they didn't want and you were a silent accomplice."

She left him with that slap of reality.

JOSH DIDN'T LIKE THIS. HE DIDN'T LIKE THIS ONE little bit. But he'd agreed to help. Even if he didn't like it. Looking to his left and then his right, he made sure no one was coming. "Almost done?"

"Just about," Eva whispered.

"Hurry up."

He glanced around again, certain that someone would catch her placing hidden cameras at any moment. This was the last one, the last hallway she was going to be spying on. At some point, someone dressed in all black would leave one condo, and Eva would be able to track her to the next condo...one where she would presumably be planting a camera. And then this would finally be over.

His stress had been heightened since she'd relayed the information she'd gathered from her talk with Neal Price. Courtney's behavior hadn't simply been to test the waters where Josh and Eva were concerned but apparently had been an attempt to break them up, break Eva's heart, and turn her into some kind of living sex toy.

He and Eva had debated how Courtney had gotten to that point, but obviously she'd been working on behalf of the Tremants. Shane and Tiffany wanted Eva. The thought made Josh's skin crawl. No, it did more than that. He was outraged.

Lusting after Eva was one thing, but actively taking such drastic steps to get to her? He'd thought that son of a bitch had crossed a dozen or more lines when he was staring at Eva in the gym. If Josh were able to, he'd beat the crap out of the man. The best he could do, though, was discreetly kill him in a way that would leave no evidence.

"Hey." Eva shook him gently. "You okay?"

He exhaled. "Yeah."

She eyed him, showing her disbelief, but then grinned. "Oh, Joshua. Were you plotting murder to protect my honor?"

"I hadn't gotten to plotting yet. I was just reminding myself that murder was an option."

"Aw, baby." Putting her hands to his cheeks, she kissed him lightly. "You're the best."

He smiled. "Are you done?"

"I am."

"Good. Now I can wow you with my computer skills."

She sighed dramatically. "I was hoping to be wowed by something else, but I'll settle for computer skills."

Putting his arm around her shoulders, he pressed the button for the elevator. Looking up, he sought out the camera she'd placed somewhere in the fake plants that adorned the hallway. "Everything's in place?"

"Yup. Let's get these cameras active and catch us a pervert."

They curbed the conversation until they returned to their condo. While Josh set up his laptop so he could connect Eva's cameras to the private website he'd set up, she scanned for any new cameras that might have been placed but didn't find any.

"There's got to be more to this," she said, plopping onto the sofa beside him.

"What do you mean?"

"I mean, this can't just be about Shane and Tiffany getting their rocks off. They get Courtney to seduce you on video, for what? To blackmail you into breaking it off with me. Then they turn around and recruit me into their little sex ring? That's an awful lot of work for a little genital gratification. There are a million websites out there with women looking for this type of situation. Shane could recruit dozens of them online. Why is he going to such lengths to manipulate the women in this building?"

"I guess he wants his own harem."

"Would you do this much work for a little bit of ass? I'm going to have Sam check the dark web again," Eva said thoughtfully. "I'd bet anything these videos are a hot commodity for some amateur porn site. The Tremants are making a killing off these women who probably don't even know they are being recorded."

"Or maybe they do. You said Courtney's room was set up like a wet dream for someone who has a schoolgirl fetish. She may be in on it."

"But I didn't find a camera in her bedroom." She scoffed. "Check that. I didn't find a hidden camera turned on and emitting a heat aura. I did not look for a hidden camera that is probably only turned on when there are activities happening. Holy shit. What is going on with these people?"

"Sex and money, babe. There's not a lot of people who won't do anything for sex and money."

"Would you do this? Have a condominium of concubines?"

"No. Jesus, Eva, most men are lucky if they can keep one woman happy. I wouldn't know what to do with two or more."

"Somehow I think you'd come up with an idea or two," she muttered.

"Look, Neal might be twisted in his justification of what he's done, but he's right on one thing. He's loyal to his wife, and whatever he's doing is to protect her. That's what a relationship is, right? You have your *one* person to love, and honor, and protect. Right? I don't need a condo building full of women." He nudged her. "I only need one."

She kissed him lightly. "You're sweet, Joshie."

His heart melted a little, even though she'd called him by *that* name. "I've been told."

Nodding her head toward his laptop, she said, "And this will store memory, right?"

"I hijacked one of the servers at HEARTS. With Sam's permission," he clarified. "She's probably the only one of you guys I can take in fisticuffs, but I don't want to risk it."

Eva chuckled. "Never underestimate a woman who wears stilettos just because."

He logged in to the site he'd created. "Do, uh, do you ever wear stilettos just because?"

"No. I do wear them for kinky sex, though."

Jerking his face to her, he stared with wide eyes. "What? We never..."

She rolled her eyes. "I haven't owned stilettos since... Never. I've never owned a single pair."

"We should fix that."

Leaning close, she brushed her chin on his shoulder and whispered, "Only if we get to buy you a gimp mask."

"What's that?"

She gawked at him for a moment before muttering under her breath about his naiveté as she Googled the term. Within a minute she was showing him the images of black leather masks, most with zippers over the mouth. "How about one of these and a studded collar so I can take you for a walk while wearing my stilettos?"

"I'll try anything once," he said, returning his attention to his task, grinning as her laughter filled the condo. "One more click here, and..." The six black boxes on his screen came to life, each one a camera showing the hallway of each floor of the building. No matter where their voyeur went, they'd be able to pinpoint her location.

Eva wrapped her arm around his back. "You are amazing, Dr. Simmons."

"Thank you, Ms. Thompson. Might I make a suggestion?"

"Snaps on your gimp mask instead of a zipper?"

He chuckled. "Chinese delivery for dinner and a long evening of monitoring the Jupiter Heights hallways so we can end this thing before someone else gets hurt."

She kissed his shoulder. "Amazing and brilliant. I'll call it in."

"I want—"

"Sweet-and-sour chicken and wonton soup."

"You know it," he said as she started scrolling through her phone again. While she ordered their dinner, Josh fine-tuned the website and used his phone to call the HEARTS office and verify with Sam that things were working on her end. This would allow any of the women to help Eva watch the hallways anytime and anywhere.

Something he definitely admired about them was how solid their team was. More like family. He had nice coworkers but definitely didn't have that kind of camaraderie with them. When he'd called in to let them know he was taking a sick day, he might as well have said he was never returning again. The one time he could recall Eva calling in sick, they had taken turns for two days staying with her while Josh went to work. He had felt like a schmuck, but Eva insisted they had more flexibly in their work than he did. Which was true, but he should have nursed her back to health. Sometimes they were both too logical for their own good.

He didn't plan to keep that pattern going, and now seemed like a good time to start surprising her. As soon as she returned to her seat and announced dinner would arrive in half an hour, he put his hand to her knee. "When this case is over, I think we should move in together."

She was surprised. Her eyes widened, and her mouth opened. "Look at you being spontaneous."

"It's not, really. It makes sense. I love you. You love me. We've already lost some time because you're so stubborn."

She gasped, and he laughed.

"Okay, because we both needed to get our heads around some things," he corrected.

"That's better."

"Maybe it seems like I'm jumping the gun here, but even after we broke up, we still"—his heart suddenly ached a little—"we still loved each other, and neither of us dated anyone else because we knew. Maybe we didn't want to admit it, but we knew. This is it."

"This is it," she said under her breath.

"So let's...jump in. Huh?"

After taking a deep breath, she nodded her agreement. "Yeah. Let's jump in."

"Your apartment is better suited, don't you think?"

One side of her mouth quirked up. "Because of my bathtub?"

"I love your bathtub," he practically growled.

She closed the distance between them to press her mouth to his. Before he could pull her deeper into the connection, her phone vibrated, and she pulled back. He wanted to protest, but she grabbed the device and had it to her ear in a split second.

"Hey, Sam."

He returned his attention to her laptop, only half listening until he caught the gist of the conversation. Sam had found what Eva had insisted was out there somewhere—amateur porn starring Shane and Tiffany Tremant. She was going to send screenshots to Eva of at least two other women to be identified. She had to find out if they knew they were being recorded and had given permission for their images to be used. If not, they were victims of a serious crime, and she had all the proof they'd need to get justice.

"I'm going to start putting the evidence together to take to the police," Eva said. She rolled her head back and nodded. "How long will that take?"

Josh squeezed her knee when she dragged her hands through her hair.

"I'll give you until noon tomorrow. Sam," she said firmly. "Noon tomorrow." Hanging up, she dropped her phone on the table and shook her head at Josh.

"She found the footage, huh?"

Eve blew out a breath. "She wants to try to trace the

account before I involve the police. She's afraid they'll take too long and the footage will disappear."

"Sounds like a legitimate concern."

"It is. But damn it." Shoving herself to her feet, she paced. "We have no way of knowing if that footage is out there with the consent of all parties involved, Josh." Stopping, she planted her hands on her hips and faced him. "If I had to place a bet on who the women are in the footage, it'd be Courtney and Brenda. I'll confirm as soon as Sam sends me a screenshot."

"Think they know?"

"Courtney might. I doubt Brenda does."

"You can't do anything about it until you hear from Sam."

Blowing out her breath, she dropped onto the sofa again. "I know."

Putting his arm around her, he pulled her closer. "Wanna look at houses?"

She laughed lightly. "Yeah. Let's look at houses."

"Yes," he said in an excited whisper. They didn't have to look at houses, and they both knew it, but if Eva didn't have a distraction, she'd lose her mind. Using the remote, Josh turned on the TV, and with a few clicks on his trackpad he transferred the output on his laptop to the large screen. With half the screen showing the hall monitors, he started searching for houses for sale on the other half.

14

As SOON AS Eva opened the locker room door, the echo of angry voices surrounded her. This was not what she'd had in mind when she'd suggested an early morning workout to Josh. She was eager to use the fancy Jupiter Heights gym one more time before handing this case over to the authorities. Breaking up a fight was not on her agenda.

"Stay away from us," one woman said.

"I didn't do anything," the other countered.

"Do you think I'm stupid, Courtney?"

"No," she deadpanned. "But it's not my fault if your boyfriend keeps coming on to me, Melly."

Ahh. Eva supposed this was inevitable. If Melly wasn't on board with the swinging game—and given the disgust she had expressed at Shane touching her ass, she never would be—it made sense that she was on the same list as Wendi Carter. "Ryan is not coming on to you. It's the other way around."

"Really?"

"I saw you, Courtney."

"You don't know what you saw." The icy chill in Courtney's tone sent a shiver down Eva's spine, encouraging her to intervene.

Rounding the row of lockers that blocked the view from the door, she didn't make her presence known as she assessed the situation. Courtney stood, hands on her hips, leaning toward the slightly shorter Melly. Melly's posture was just as threatening, with her finger pointed in Courtney's face and a fist clenched at her side.

"Stay away from Ryan."

"Tell him to stay away from me."

"I thought you were my friend," Melly said.

Courtney tilted her head and pouted. "Aw, that's adorable, Mel."

"You're crazy."

Courtney took a step closer, glaring down at Melly. "What did you say?"

"Ladies?" Eva asked, concerned a fistfight was about to break out.

Melly looked at Eva immediately, but Courtney continued her death glare for a good five seconds before backing down.

"This doesn't concern you," Courtney said. Every little bit of the sweet façade she'd displayed previously was gone. Anger showed plainly in her set jaw and narrowed eyes.

"Maybe it does." Eva didn't take her eyes off Courtney, keeping alert in case she displayed any further signs of aggression. "Sounds like you threw yourself at Ryan just like you did Joshua."

Melly let out a bitter laugh. "You fucking whore. Is there anyone in this building you haven't tried to sleep with?" Turning her attention to Eva, she smirked. "She even tried to screw me. She got me drunk and suggested we try on some of her clothes. Before I could get out of one outfit and into another, she had her hand on my crotch and her tongue in my mouth." Glaring at Courtney, she shook her head. "She blamed it on the liquor, but I think she's just a slut."

"Or maybe I was just verifying you're a vanilla bitch. Ryan's imagination must be extraordinary to be able to get off with your boring ass."

"Okay." Eva waved her hand, indicating for Melly to come close. "Come on. Let's go before this gets any uglier than it already has."

A wicked sneer played across Courtney's face as Melly joined Eva. "Oh, it's just getting started."

"Yes," Eva stated firmly. "It certainly is."

The locker room door had barely closed behind them before tears spilled down Melly's cheeks. "I hate her."

"I know. But trust that she'll get what's coming to her."

Dragging the back of her hand under her eyes, she released a shaky breath. "Watch out for her. She'll screw anyone. I actually caught her fucking Tiffany Tremant in the hot tub."

Melly's statement was met with a dramatic gasp. Eva

glanced over her shoulder at Brenda Price, who had, at some point, walked into the open area outside the gym where men went to the right to change and women to the left.

Brenda's jaw slacked and her face paled under the clear overhead lights. "Who? Who's sleeping with Tiffany?"

The locker room door squeaked as it opened and Courtney walked through.

Oh no.

Melly's sense of vengeance was palpable as she pointed. "That skank right there."

Eva practically dove in front of Courtney to stop Brenda from attacking. She put a hand up to both women, but her attempt was futile. Brenda seemed to embrace her inner feral cat and lunged, claws out, looking as if she were ready to rip Courtney's face off. The sounds tearing from her throat were not normal. Nor was the way she swung her arms at everything but nothing in particular. Eva did her best not to get hit, but a nail dragged down her cheek.

The pain set off her protective reflexes. Wrapping her arm around Brenda's, she twisted until Brenda cried out dramatically and bent forward. Eva was practiced enough in the move to know she wasn't really hurting her. A little pinch in the shoulder that would ease the moment she released her.

"Calm down," she ordered.

"Let go of me, you lunatic."

"Brenda," Eva said in an even tone. "Take a few deep breaths and calm down."

She did as she was told, and Eva eased her hold. Standing up, she glared as she rubbed her shoulder joint. "I should have you arrested."

Eva wiped her cheek and then held her fingers up to show the streak of blood. "I was defending myself."

Looking beyond Eva, Brenda glared as her lip trembled. "Is it true?" she asked Courtney. "Are you with Tiffany?"

Courtney smirked but didn't answer. She stared Brenda down as she sashayed by, letting her cockiness be the only response given. Even without the words, Brenda got the message loud and clear.

"Tiff wouldn't do that to me. She wouldn't," Brenda insisted.

Eva guided her back into the locker room and eased her onto a bench. Melly joined them, looking shocked into silence as Brenda lowered her face and sobbed quietly.

"She promised to wait until I could leave Neal. She said she loved me."

Eva caught Melly's gaze. "Would you go let Josh know I'll be a few minutes?"

She opened her mouth as if to argue but snapped her lips shut and left.

Once alone, Eva leaned against the door to stop anyone else from entering. "Maybe she thought that at some point in time, but her actions indicate that she and Shane have made other plans."

Darting her teary eyes up, she creased her brow. "What does Shane have to do with this?"

Eva debated how much to share. "Tiffany took me shopping one day. She didn't particularly care what clothing I liked; she picked out what she liked. Then she took me to her salon and had my hair dyed and cut in a style she chose."

"*No*," she whispered.

"Do you know why?"

Brenda closed her eyes and swallowed so hard the gulping sound bounced around the locker room.

"You told me once to be careful because I was 'their' type. Did you mean Shane and Tiffany?"

Giving her head a hard shake, she looked at Eva. "No."

"Who did you mean?"

"What does it matter?"

"It matters. If Tiffany Tremant was grooming me to be her and her husband's sex toy, I'd like to know."

Brenda wiped her face. "When I said that, I meant Shane and Neal. I...I had an affair. With Tiffany. Obviously." Exhaling, she dried her hands on her workout shorts. "Shane and Tiffany... They were open to..."

"Swinging," Eva offered. She didn't particularly care for Brenda, but seeing her uncomfortable didn't exactly make her happy. The woman deserved a little of her dignity spared.

She blushed but didn't deny the suggestion. "Neal

was furious. I don't know why. He'd been sleeping around, too. He just wouldn't admit it."

Well, that was news. "With whom?"

She scoffed. "Everyone. You think every bitch in this building looks like a stripper by coincidence?" She pressed her lips together. "No offense."

"None taken."

"Neal got all bent out of shape when I cheated, but he cheated, too. And as far as I can tell, he still is."

"Why do you say that?"

Brenda gestured toward Eva. "You're fucking him, aren't you?"

"No," she stated without hesitation.

"Don't lie," she said under her breath. "I see how you watch him."

Eva couldn't deny watching him. She'd been suspicious of him from the day he'd hired her. "Mrs. Price. *Brenda*. I have never slept with your husband. I am one hundred percent devoted to my boyfriend."

"Is he devoted to you?"

"Yes. Courtney tried to turn his head, and he made it clear to her, and to me, he isn't interested."

She sniffed, her shoulders sagging as if she'd just given up hope of ever getting out of sharing her darkest secrets. "Has Neal ever come on to you?"

"No."

"Has Shane?"

"He likes to stare at me from afar, but he's never directly tried to approach me."

"Give him time. The only reason I was willing to swing with the Tremants was so I could be with Tiffany. Shane is sleazy, but if I had to let him touch me so I could be with her, I was willing to do that. But Neal refused and said if he found out I was with them, he'd divorce me. I didn't care. But Tiffany and I needed time to put money away so we could leave together. At first we'd meet once a week at a hotel and spend a few hours. We'd talk about the future. Then she started making excuses why she couldn't meet with me. Then she just stopped responding to me altogether. Now she won't even look at me when we run into each other. Now I find out..." She sobbed. "She's been sleeping with Courtney."

"When did you start to suspect Neal was cheating on you?"

"A long time ago, but after he found out about me and Tiffany, he stopped being so careful."

"What do you mean?"

"He says he's playing golf or going for a jog. A jog? He's twenty pounds overweight. He hasn't jogged in years. I'm not stupid. I sneaked into his office and looked at his key fob records. He wasn't even leaving the property. I know what he's doing, I just don't know who he is doing it with." She clenched her jaw. "Once I get proof, I can divorce him and his evidence of me sleeping with Tiffany will be null and void. Tit for tat, right?"

Eva was glad she and Holly had insisted that he draw up a fake contract. They had suspected the voyeur was an insider and wanted to be damn sure the truth behind Eva living in the condo wasn't exposed. Good damn thing. She let Brenda's reasoning fall by the wayside; she was more interested in something else. "Exactly how did you plan to get proof?"

She straightened, shifted. "I have someone watching him."

"How are they watching him?"

She shrugged. "I didn't ask. I just told her I'd pay for evidence."

Eva stood upright. "*Her?*"

Brenda snapped her lips shut and shoved herself to her feet. "I need to go."

Lifting her hand, Eva indicated for her to stop. "Her who?"

"It doesn't matter."

"It matters more than you realize. Who is getting evidence for you? *Mrs. Price.*"

Lifting her chin, looking down her nose at Eva, Brenda stated, "I don't have to tell you that. I don't have to tell you anything. And if I find out you're spreading gossip about me, Tiffany, *or* Courtney, I'll make your life at Jupiter Heights so miserable you'll have no choice but to move. Don't think I won't."

Eva didn't give a shit about her life at Jupiter Heights, but she could understand how that threat might intimidate some of the other women in the building. This location was prime market and not easy to come by. The prestige of living in this area was far more important to some young professionals than it should be. Image was everything for those climbing corporate ladders, and living in a top-of-the-market condominium created a very impressive image. Eva, however, could not care less.

She blocked the door before Brenda could leave. "By what means is she getting evidence?"

"I don't know."

"Why is she helping you?"

She scoffed. "Because she has just as much to gain by my leaving Neal as I do."

Seriously? Yet another forbidden romance? Did these people ever keep their clothes on?

"Who is she?" Eva pressed.

"Get out of my way."

Eva didn't budge. "Your little spy is in a lot of trouble, Brenda. She's been hiding cameras all over this building."

"Placing cameras isn't illegal."

"Breaking and entering is."

Brenda paled again. She even swayed a little on her feet.

"My boyfriend found a hidden camera in our kitchen just a day or so after he was assaulted and had his keys stolen. Do you know how many charges your friend faces if I call the police?" She held up one finger. "Assault and battery." A second finger. "Petty theft." A third finger. "Breaking and entering." A fourth finger. "Invasion of privacy. Now, you can tell me who she is and let me deal with her, or I can call the police and let them handle it."

Brenda started for the door again. This time Eva let her go. She'd planted the seed of panic; now all she had to do was give it some time to grow. The moment Brenda confronted whomever she was working with about the crimes she'd committed, she was bound to try to retrieve any remaining cameras she'd hidden in the building.

And Eva would catch her with her own hidden cameras.

Sometimes karma coming back around felt too damn good.

JOSHUA DIDN'T USE THE WORD HATE LIGHTLY, BUT HE *hated* Shane Tremant. The meathead kept smirking at him the way jocks used to in high school before shoving him into a locker. He wasn't as much of a victim these days. Josh met Shane's gaze in the mirror for what was probably the twentieth time since he'd entered the gym. Instead of looking away, pretending he hadn't read Shane's aggressive body language, Josh returned his stare. And Shane's smirk grew.

As unsettling as Shane's behavior was, Josh was more worried about how long it was taking Eva to join him. Since he'd been attacked in the men's locker room, she'd opted to put their keys and her phone—his still was missing—in the women's locker room. She hadn't joined him yet. He reminded himself that she could handle any situation that arose, but he was fighting the urge to check on her. And the more Shane acted like he was up to something, the more concerned Josh grew about what was keeping Eva.

He put down the hand weights he'd been lifting, deciding enough time had passed that he could check on her without it being viewed as him not being confident in her abilities. He was almost to the door when the thing he was dreading presented itself.

"Where's your girl?" Shane asked.

Josh stopped in his tracks and turned slowly. "Excuse me?"

The man licked his lips and grabbed his crotch as uncouth men tended to do. "Eva. She coming to work out?"

A rage sparked in Josh that he'd never felt before. In all his years, all the horrible things he'd seen in the morgue and at crime scenes, he'd never felt anger like what started boiling low in his gut. "Don't say her name."

Shane's smile widened. "Whose name? Eva's?" Mischief danced in his eyes as he licked his lips again. "My wife really likes her. Says her tits are some of the perkiest she's ever seen."

Josh knew bullies. He'd dealt with them most of his youth. He'd learned long ago that walking away was the best way to deal with situations like this, but this bastard had crossed a line Josh wasn't willing to walk away from. Sexualizing Eva was not okay.

"I think they might be the second perkiest I've ever seen, but I'll let you know for sure once I get a better look."

Crossing the small gym, Josh got as close to Shane as he could without having to crane his neck back to look up at him. The man was at least six inches taller, and his muscle mass probably made three of Josh. He didn't care. He wasn't concerning himself with the ass-beating he'd take. He would defend Eva to the death if he had to.

Shane actually laughed and then stood straighter as veins in his neck started to bulge. "Might want to just stand down, peewee. A woman like that needs a real man. One who can show her a real good time."

The image that flashed through Josh's mind—Shane pushing himself on Eva—flipped a switch. Logic gone, Josh balled his fists and charged the much larger man. And it was high school all over again. He was in a head-lock, throwing fists that landed on meaty flesh but had no real impact, as Shane laughed.

Grabbing a fist of Josh's hair, Shane shoved him down as he kicked his feet out from under him. Josh landed face-down on the padded gym floor. The old Josh told him to stay down, but there was no way this pig was going to get away with sexually harassing Eva like that. Pushing himself up in a fluid motion like Eva had taught him, Josh tightened his fists in a defensive posture.

"Real men don't talk about women like that," he said to Shane's back.

Shane turned and smiled. "Well, look at you, peewee. You got a little fire in you." His smile faded as he used his right fist to punch his left palm three times. "I can fix that."

"Bring it on," Josh said with a confidence he definitely didn't feel.

"I can take you down in one punch."

"Try it."

Shane rotated his neck to the right, and the sound of popping joints filled the room, even over the deep bass pumping out of the hidden speakers. "First," he said, "I'm going to take care of you." He rotated his neck to the left with the same effect. "Then I'm going to take care of that poor girl who's been stuck with a weasel like you."

"Eva knows what you're all about. You make her sick."

Shane's eyes hardened. His amusement was gone. "What the fuck does that mean?"

"She's this close to getting all the evidence she needs to expose you." The words were out before Josh realized their repercussions. Shit. He was shaken. And he'd done it to himself. He stuttered, betraying his false bravado.

That little moment of weakness was all Shane needed to go for the figurative kill. He stopped showing off his superior physicality and grabbed Josh again. Fisting his shirt, he lifted until Josh had to get on his tiptoes. "Tell me what you meant before I break you in half, you little twig."

In that moment, Josh decided if he was getting his ass kicked, he would at least get a few jabs in. "I know that you have to manipulate women, lie to them, break them down so they'll join your little harem. And you call yourself a real man. You're no better than a pimp on the street."

That was probably not the best decision. Shane

slammed his fist into Josh's ribs. The air left Josh's lungs as he grunted.

"Who have you been talking to?" Shaking Josh, he forced him to look eye to eye again. "Who have you been talking to?"

Shane pulled his fist back, this time aiming for Josh's face.

"Boys?" Eva called. "Is there a problem?"

Of course she'd walk in right then. At Josh's worst possible moment. But he supposed it could be worse; at least his face was still in one piece.

Shane jerked Josh. "We're just playing. Ain't we, boy?"

"Fuck off," Josh squeezed out.

"Get your hands off him." Eva's cold voice echoed around the gym.

"Sure thing," Shane said as his taunting smirk mocked Josh. "For a kiss."

Josh tensed and swung his fists. Shane didn't seem to feel the impact.

"Come get it," Eva said in that deep, sexy tone she used in the bedroom.

Hearing that now infuriated Josh even more. That was the voice she saved for him. He didn't think for a moment that she was going to let Shane Tremant kiss her, but damn it, she shouldn't let someone else hear *that* tone.

Even so, Josh took some joy in knowing she was going to make Shane rue the day he'd decided manipulating women for sex was okay.

He let go of Josh's shirt and ruffled his hair. "Might want to take notes, peewee. I'm about to give your girl what she's been missing."

Josh sneered. "Or maybe she'll give you what you've been deserving."

The challenge, though he couldn't possibly understand it, clearly thrilled Shane. He shoved Josh away and took four big strides to stop in front of Eva. He was taking his last step when she made her move. Shane had at least a foot on Eva, and one thing she'd taught Josh was to bring the attacker to his level. She did that by sideswiping Shane's knee with the inside of her foot. He stumbled, and she had her arms around his neck, squeezing him in a headlock that made him swing his arms. Moving behind him to avoid his punches, she tightened her hold until Shane gagged. Then he dropped to his knees. Seconds later, he passed out and fell limp to the floor.

Untangling herself, she stood upright and frowned at Josh. "What have I told you about roughhousing?"

He barely heard her question. "What happened to your face?"

She touched her wound. "Brenda Price is a bit of a hellcat. And you?"

He winced at the pain in his side. "He said things about you I didn't like."

"What things?"

"Things that a boyfriend should defend."

"Aw, Joshie." She closed the distance between them. "Did he hurt you?"

"No," he lied. His ribs were probably cracked. Breathing was almost as painful as moving. He looked at the scratch on her face. "I should clean that."

"Later. I'm more concerned about you." She tilted her head and gave him sad eyes. "Are you sure he didn't hurt you?"

"Well, maybe a little."

"Baby," she cooed. Sliding her hands up his arms, she kissed him lightly. "You sure are taking a lot of damage this week."

He rested his palms on her hips, soaking up her sympathy. Eva didn't pamper him often, but when she did, it usually led to *really* good things. Even if his ribs hurt and his face was still bruised, the pain was worth what he anticipated the payoff in the bedroom would be. "Just doing my part to help you."

"I appreciate it more than you know." She pressed her lips to his again but pulled back when Shane coughed. She turned from Josh as the man at their feet got onto his knees and rubbed his neck.

He looked up, narrowing his eyes at her. "Who are you?"

"Joshua's girlfriend."

"You a cop?"

"No."

He rubbed his neck where she'd choked him. "Fed?"

"No."

Turning his neck, he popped his joints. Joshua fought the urge to tell him that doing so too frequently could lead to perpetual instability which, in turn, increased his risk of developing osteoarthritis.

Rolling his head back, Shane eyed Eva again but jerked his chin toward Josh. "He said you have some kind of evidence on me."

Josh held his breath. Oh. Shit. He did say that. And he would have told her about it. Eventually.

Eva said, "You must have misunderstood."

"I didn't."

"Stay down," Eva warned when he started to stand.

He chuckled. "Spoken like a pig." Shane stood, wavered a bit as his blood started cycling properly, and then looked between them. "I don't care who you are. You don't have anything on me because I haven't done anything. Stay the fuck away from me."

He left the gym, and Eva turned on her heels, her jaw set as she stared at Josh. He lifted his hands, but before he could defend himself, she leaned in.

"What did you say?"

"I-I don't remember exactly."

"Then summarize."

"He, uh, he made comments about...sleeping with you, and I-I lost it, Eva."

She didn't look impressed by his excuse. "What did you tell him, Joshua?"

"I said you knew what he was about, and he made you sick. And..."

"And?"

He winced at his own stupidity. "And that...you're this close to busting him."

"Fuck," she spat. Stepping away from him, she ran her hand over her head before glaring at him. "You're an idiot, Joshua!"

"Eva."

"You could have just blown everything I've been working on."

He tried to apologize, but she stormed out, leaving him standing there, knee deep in a shitstorm of his own making.

15

Eva had to walk away from Josh before she killed him. His misstep with Tremant proved the point she'd been trying to make all along. He wasn't a PI, and he didn't have any business being so involved in her case. He damned well better not have just ruined all the strides she'd made in nailing down the voyeur.

In the locker room, she grabbed her keys and phone from her locker and slammed the door open, part of her hoping Josh was standing on the other side so she could bash his face again.

She crossed the lobby in a few long strides and pressed the button to the elevator. Thankfully she didn't have to wait long for the doors to slide open. She started to step in and nearly ran into Cody. Eva was sure she heard the girl mutter something about Eva being a stupid bitch as she passed, but Eva didn't have the energy to give a shit about the moody teenager.

She was over this case. Over these people. Over the bedroom-hopping and the significant-other-stealing ways of this condominium. She wanted to be done with everything that seemed to be going on in this building so she could put some damned space between her and Josh.

That would be easier said than done. She shouldn't have slept with him. She never should have slept with him, but she definitely shouldn't have gone back there. How many more ways did he need to prove they were not compatible? How many more ways did she need to see that they did not work well together before she stopped trying to imagine them having some great life that would never come to be?

Unlocking the door to her condo, she immediately sensed something was off. Her Spidey sense, as Alexa called it, went into high alert. Instead of slamming the door as she had intended, she eased it shut with barely a click. Since the condo was an open-concept layout, she could see the majority of the space was empty. That left the bedroom—where her gun was locked in a safe in the nightstand—and the bathroom as the two likely hiding places.

The door behind her opened, and she spun, hands raised, ready to defend herself. Josh walked in. She put her finger to her lips, hushing him before he could speak. He opened his mouth, and she was tempted to slap him, but a noise from the bedroom drew her attention. Josh was all but forgotten as she started toward the back of the condo.

She was closing in on the doorway when a tall, thin blonde backed out.

"Sam," Eva reprimanded.

The woman squealed as she spun around, hand to her chest and eyes wide. "Shit, Eva. You scared me."

"You're lucky I didn't do worse. What are you doing?"

"You weren't answering my calls, and when I got here, the door was open. I was worried."

"The door was open?" Eva clarified.

"Yeah. I was afraid something had happened to you."

Eva glanced at Josh. He didn't have to speak. She knew they'd closed the door on the way downstairs. "Did it look like anything was disturbed?"

"No."

Even so, Eva stuck her head in the bedroom and bathroom, and skimmed the kitchen. Then she noticed Josh's laptop. The numerous blocks, the ones that had been constantly streaming the hallways, were black. "What the hell? Josh, what's wrong with the cameras?"

He dropped onto the sofa and started clicking and typing and switching screens. "They're not connected to the Wi-Fi." He looked up at her. "I think someone turned them off."

"Can you review the footage?"

He selected the camera that Eva had placed in the hallway on their floor and backed up the footage until a figure appeared, searched through the fake tree where the camera was planted, and snagged the camera. This time, however, it wasn't a petite female. This time the offender didn't hide *his* face. This time it was clearly Neal Price.

"What the hell?" Eva demanded. "Go back to see who opened our door."

They watched as Neal walked down the hallway, pounded on Eva and Josh's door several times, and then dug a set of keys from his pocket.

"Son of a bitch," Eva muttered.

Neal let himself in and few moments later practically ran out and started scouring through the tree.

"I didn't even notice the laptop was still on," Josh said. "I'm sorry, Eva."

She shook her head. She didn't even know what to say. "This case is blown. The only chance we have now is convincing Brenda to talk, and good luck getting her to turn on her lover."

"Wait," Sam called when she turned to go confront the man who'd hired her. "I'd been trying to reach you because I traced the credit card associated with the Dark Web account that uploaded the videos with the Tremants."

"Shane?" Eva asked.

Sam shook her head. "Neal Price."

Eva creased her brow and took a breath. "What the hell is going on around here? I'm going to get some damn answers."

"Eva?" Sam said. "Maybe change?"

Looking down at her bralette and short shorts, she nodded. "Did you scan for cameras?"

"No."

Instead of taking the time, distracting her from her mission, she pulled a pair of jeans and a dark shirt over her gym attire. She put her gun holster on her belt, checked her Beretta, and slid it into place. "Sam. Scan while I'm gone," she instructed, shrugging into the little black jacket that hid her gun from view.

"Where are you going?" Josh asked.

She cast a frown his way, but that was the only response she gave him. Turning her attention back to Sam, she asked, "Do you have the report on the Dark Web account?"

Wide-eyed, Sam looked between Eva and Josh before grabbing a file off the kitchen counter and holding it out.

After skimming through the information Sam had gathered, Eva grabbed her messenger bag from beside the sofa and opened it. Her breath caught. "My notebook is gone. Goddamn it!" Throwing her bag down, she exhaled.

"All your reports are up-to-date at the office," Sam offered. "I type up all the meeting notes every day."

Eva nodded, muttered her thanks, and then glared at Josh one more time. Dumbass.

With her anger fully engaged, she stormed out of the condo on her way to confront Neal and Brenda Price one more time. She was done playing games with these people. All of them. She knew what the hell she was doing and what she should have done all along. Why had she pussy-footed around with this case? Josh. That was why. She'd been distracted playing house with her stupid ex. Well, that was done now. And so was she. This case was getting resolved now.

Instead of taking the elevator, she climbed the flight of stairs to the fourth floor and headed straight to the Prices' condo. She banged on the door and waited. And waited. Then banged again. After the third round of pounding her fist against the hard surface, the door was opened.

Brenda peered out, her eyes wet and her nose red. "Go away."

"I have everything I need to get the police involved. If you don't open the door, right now, I'll do just that." She held up her phone just in case Brenda wanted to call her bluff.

Stepping back, Brenda opened the door and gestured Eva in. Eva scanned the room, making sure she was aware of any potential dangers but also noting how the room looked like someone's mood board vomited over the space. Whitewashed furniture, fake vintage signs on the walls, and varying shades of white, blue, and gray filled the space.

Staying close to the door, Eva met Brenda's gaze. "Is anyone else here?"

Brenda shook her head.

"Did you speak to Neal about our discussion?"

She sniffed. "What makes you think—"

"Can you cut the bullshit, Brenda?"

"You first."

Eva stared her down for a few beats. "A resident in

this building found a hidden camera in her condo last week. I was hired to find out who placed it."

"I know. Neal told me who you were when I confronted him."

"Confronted him?"

"None of this would have happened if he'd just..."

"Let you screw around?"

"Been more reasonable." She swallowed hard and sniffed. "I want to leave my husband, but he has evidence of my affair."

"You said."

"I needed evidence of my own."

Eva nodded and did her best not to roll her eyes at the woman. "Yeah. I know this. What I don't know is who is getting that evidence."

"I am." She lifted her chin a notch. "I hid the cameras."

"You hid the cameras?"

"Yes."

Eva didn't have to be a PI to know this woman was lying to protect the real culprit. "You hid the camera next to my microwave?"

"Yes."

Uh-huh. "And the one in my bedroom?"

"Yes."

Sure you did. "And the one in the women's locker room?"

Brenda inhaled a slow breath. "Yes."

Crossing her arms, Eva scowled. "There was no camera in the locker room or my bedroom. The camera in my kitchen was nowhere near the microwave. Who are you protecting?"

She creased her brow for a millisecond before digging her heels in. "No one. I did it. I wanted to catch Neal screwing around."

Eva sighed. "Did you also upload videos onto an amateur porn site?"

Brenda's face paled. Eva opened the file to show her a screenshot of the account Sam had traced back to Neal's credit card. Next she showed her the screenshots Sam had printed off. In one, Brenda's and Tiffany's faces were clear, easily identifiable, as was the sex act they were engaging in. The second was of a naked Tiffany lying on top of a naked Courtney on Courtney's oversize sofa. Shane wasn't seen in either image, but Sam had indicated that he'd made an appearance in at least one of the videos on the site.

Brenda nearly missed the sofa as she dropped to sit. "Oh. My. God."

"I'm guessing that's a no," Eva said. Part of her thought she should feel some sympathy for this woman who had just lied to her, but she couldn't. She wasn't exactly innocent in the events happening around her.

Covering her mouth, she choked on a cry as another round of tears fell. She turned the pictures over and closed her eyes. She'd clearly had no idea someone had uploaded the evidence of her affair online. "That little bitch. I actually believed her when she said she'd been taking money from her savings account."

Eva took time to wrap her mind around the implications of Brenda's words. "You said your partner in crime had just as much to gain by getting you out of this marriage as you did. I assumed you meant a lover."

Brenda didn't seem to hear her. She was staring at the photos.

"You told me the other day that Neal was concerned about the money your daughter was coming into. You resented being forced into helicopter-parenting a teenager. I don't suppose during all your hovering, you restricted her access to the Internet?"

Brenda shook her head as another cry ripped from her chest.

"The website has been traced back to Neal's credit card. Would anyone else have access to that?"

"I told you he's been sleeping around. Anybody could have used his card. How would I know who?"

"Why on earth would you ask your daughter to get evidence of her father cheating?"

Brenda's lips quivered until she pressed them together. "Cody heard Neal and me fighting one night. She was so mad at me for having an affair, but she had no idea how cruel Neal could be. I'd always been a buffer between them. After he got his hands on that video, he decided he got to make all the decisions and I had to go along with everything. We no longer talk about what is best or what we should do. He just decides. He pulled strings to get Cody accepted at this elite school. She hates it. She just wants to go back to her regular school to be with her friends, but he won't hear of it. She got so mad one night, she said it was all my fault because I was with Tiffany. I told her if we got divorced..." Her face squished into an ugly cry as she seemed to finally understand the drama she'd unleashed. "I told her he wouldn't have a say in what school she attended because I'd have custody of her, but I couldn't do that until I had evidence that he had cheated, too. I had no idea she'd so something like this."

Okay. Now Eva felt badly for her. "Brenda," she said softly. "Why would Cody put a video of you on the Internet?"

"I don't know. Maybe she got mad when she saw me with Tiffany?"

"What did you say to Neal after we talked in the locker room?"

"I told him it was his fault that Cody put hidden cameras in your condo. He went down to fire you before you could figure out it was her. We thought if we could get you out of the way, we could make all this go away."

And then he'd gone into her condo when she hadn't answered and noticed the camera feed. Damn it.

"I saw Cody earlier. Do you know where she was headed?"

"I don't know."

"She could be in real legal trouble here, Brenda. Call her now. We need to find out exactly what she's done so we can minimize the damage."

"Are you going to turn her in?"

Without a doubt. The girl had uploaded porn onto the Internet without the consent of the participants. "Let's get all the answers before we decide how to move forward. Do you mind if I look through her room while we wait for her?"

Brenda didn't answer. She seemed to be rolling all the possible outcomes through her mind.

"Look, I'm not out to get Cody. If she did this, she is going to have to face the consequences. But maybe she didn't. Maybe all this evidence pointing at her can be explained."

Finally Brenda gestured to the door to the right at the back of the apartment. "Go ahead."

Eva gathered the images back into her folder and walked into the dark-painted bedroom. The twin bed in the corner was angled so Cody would be able to see out the windows by leaning against the headboard. The built-in desk had big speakers and a PC with two monitors. Of course the desktop was password protected. She'd have to get Cody to log in if she decided to push the girl. She might just call the PD and hand this case over. Let them decide how to handle it. Her assessment that she was over this case still stood.

She opened drawers and shuffled the contents. She wasn't completely sure what she was looking for, but if there were other missing elements of this case, she wanted to figure them out before bringing in the police.

Her search ended when the front door slammed.

"What have you done?" Brenda screeched.

"I didn't do anything," Cody protested.

"Hidden cameras, Cody?"

"I don't—"

"Don't lie to me!"

Easing into the living room, Eva watched the two standing in a confrontation. Cody noticed Eva and glared.

Cody didn't take her evil stare from Eva as she asked her mother, "What is she doing here?"

"She's an investigator! She knows what you've done."

Cody's eyes widened, and she shook her head. "I didn't do anything."

"Cody," Eva started.

"Fuck you!"

Brenda took such a deep breath, her back arched unnaturally. "Young lady, you are in big trouble here."

"You need to talk to me," Eva pressed.

Cody narrowed her eyes and opened her mouth. Eva lifted her hands in the way that Holly did when she was trying to maintain or regain control. Amazingly, it worked, and Cody snapped her mouth shut.

"Just answer a few questions for me, okay?"

Brenda pushed her daughter to the couch and muttered for her to sit. Cody did, and when she looked up, the tough-girl exterior cracked and tears filled her eyes.

"Cody," Eva said softly, "I've talked to your mom. I know you thought you were helping her."

Cody sniffed and wiped her nose with the cuff of her sweatshirt. "I didn't do anything for her." She jerked her shoulders to shake Brenda's hand off her shoulder. Looking at her mother, she gave her the evil look. "You make me sick. Both of you do."

"I know what you saw—"

"Was twisted."

Brenda flinched. "Tiffany and I..."

"That's not what I'm talking about. Like I give a shit who you're screwing."

Creasing her brow, her confusion evident, Brenda said, "Then what do you mean?"

"Melly told me all about it." Her voice cracked more with each word. "How you and Dad and the Tremants select women to live here. How you like them to look the same so you can all have sex with them. You've turned Jupiter Heights into your own personal whorehouse."

Whoa.

"What?" Brenda practically screeched.

"Look at her!" She pointed at Eva. "She looks like a fucking doll. You and Dad—"

"I had nothing to do with that! Why the hell do you think I'm trying to get us out of here, Cody? I can't leave him—"

"Yes, I heard your excuse, Mother."

"It's not an excuse," she whispered. "What am I going to do without your dad's income? How will I take care of you?"

"I found a way to take care of myself."

"By selling pornography online?" Brenda spat.

Cody gawked at her. "What?"

"Show her," she demanded of Eva.

Eva held the folder up. "I'm not sharing those images with a child."

Brenda stared at her before finally conceding. "Someone put hidden cameras all over the building. And you know what happened to that footage? It was uploaded onto a porn site. And do you know who Eva tracked that website back to? *You.*"

Cody's face paled. "No. That's not what I did. Mom! I didn't do that."

"Then where did all this money come from all the sudden, Cody? Your dad thought you were selling drugs."

"I set up a website for Melly and showed her how to access it. I mean, yeah, I did use Dad's credit card for the bill so I could pocket the cash she paid me. But it isn't for porn."

Eva frowned. How low could Melly sink? Using a teenager to cover her tracks.

"Are you sure about that?" Brenda asked. "How do you know it isn't for porn?"

Cody jumped up and marched into her room. Brenda and Eva stood back as she typed in her password and opened the browser. With a few taps on her keyboard, she brought up a website for a romance book readers' club.

Cody gestured to the screen. "Does this look like porn to you?"

At first glance, no, it didn't. But to Eva's trained eye, it only took a moment to notice that all was not as it seemed.

"Cody, turn the volume down and stand over there with your back to us, please."

After she did as she was told, Eva started clicking on the options on the products. The more she clicked, going deeper into the descriptions, the murkier the site got. Finally she clicked on a tag that read "Triad." There, the page changed to an unlisted page offering a variety of threesome videos. Brenda gasped.

"What?" Cody asked.

"Don't you turn around," Brenda warned. She moved to block the girl's view. "That bitch used my daughter."

Eva took a breath. The female voyeur, the one she'd caught on video placing cameras, wasn't Tiffany, Brenda, or Cody. It was fucking Melly.

"Why would she do this?" Brenda demanded.

Thinking back on the confrontation in the locker room, she sighed. "Because she figured it out. Like Cody said. She figured out Neal and Shane were bringing in a specific type of woman. Courtney was trying to break up Melly and her boyfriend and likely pull her into their lifestyle. She knew about it, and instead of exposing it, she decided to make money off their manipulations."

"But why put me up there? I didn't do anything to her."

"You're Neal's wife. She probably assumes you're in on this, too."

"I want that bitch in jail."

"I'm sure you aren't alone in that," Eva said. "I'm going to need you both to come with me."

Brenda instantly grew aggressive. "You're not arresting my daughter."

"I'm not arresting anyone. I'm not a cop. But I am an investigator who can help you so she doesn't get arrested. I need to know everything, from the beginning, Cody, so I can try to get you out of this mess. Now, come with me. I need to get my keys and take you to my office. I'll sit with you and help you work out the details before the police get involved."

"Do we have to involve the cops?" Cody whined.

"You set up a website. You didn't know what the content was really going to be, but yes, we have to involve the cops. Melly putting revenge porn on the Internet is illegal. You were unknowingly used, but you are a witness to a crime and the police will want to hear from you. I can make this much more comfortable for you. If you want me to."

Brenda and Cody looked at each other before Brenda finally nodded. "Yes. We'd like that."

JOSH SAT, FINGERS ENTWINED AS HE STARED AT HIS laptop. Man, he'd blown it. Big-time blown it. He didn't stop staring at the blank screens until Sam held out a cup of tea. "Thanks," he muttered.

"Eva will come around," she offered.

Josh shook his head. "I don't know. I really screwed this up for her. She was right. I never did belong here."

Sitting beside him, she gave him a gentle bump and then gasped when he winced. "Sorry. Sorry. I forgot about your ribs."

He groaned. "No. I deserved that."

"Oh, come on, Josh. Once she calms down, she's going to see that you didn't do any of this on purpose. You're not trained to think like she is. Your brain isn't always trying to stay ahead of the situation so you can see what's coming before anyone else. Listen," she said gently, "I get it. I know what it feels like to be on the outside of this group. They are scary smart. I actually have had nightmares about being interrogated by them. They are intimidating as hell, and trying to fit in with them is hard. Not because they don't have their arms open to us but because we aren't like them. You tried too hard. That's all. You just tried too hard."

"It wasn't that, Sam. I got overprotective of Eva and spoke without thinking of the consequences."

"Okay. So she'll understand that, too."

"No, she won't."

A pounding against the door made them both jump. Josh put his hand to his ribcage as he stood. Seeing Neal Price through the peephole, he debated whether he should answer. Looking over his shoulder, he frowned at Sam. "Let Eva know Price is here."

Sam pulled her phone from her pocket as he opened the door. He was about invite Price in when Shane Tremant shoved him aside and grabbed Josh.

Crap!

"Where is it?" Lifting Josh off his feet by his shirtfront, Shane carried him into the condo. He dropped him with enough of a shove that Josh stumbled backward.

Sam had jumped up and now grabbed Josh's arm, helping him find his balance. "What the hell are you doing?" she demanded.

"Who are you?"

"She's one of them," Neal Price said. "She works for the PI."

Josh put himself between Sam and Tremant. As if he could protect her. He'd more than proven that he wasn't up for that task, but the way Shane was glaring at them, he was going to at least try to defend his friend. Josh might not be musclebound or trained in martial arts, but he wasn't the pushover that men like Shane Tremant and Neal Price seemed to think he was. Balling his fists, he lifted them, ready to fight.

Shane laughed. "Didn't get enough earlier, huh?" His smile faded, and fury filled his eyes. "I want whatever evidence that bitch has. Then I'll leave."

"I don't know what you mean." Josh deliberately cast his eyes toward his laptop, just a quick glance that was enough to distract Shane.

Shane turned his attention to the computer on the coffee table. When he headed that way with Neal Price following behind, Josh grabbed Sam's arm and pulled her toward the door. They were almost there when a loud banging rang out. Josh ducked, and Sam squealed. They both turned to see what was happening and watched as

Shane smashed Josh's laptop against the corner of the coffee table several more times, effectively destroying it.

"Damn it," Neal cursed. "This is going too far, Shane."

"I'm not going to jail because your stupid ass hired a two-bit PI."

"Shush," Sam whispered before Josh could counter Shane's assessment.

He snapped his lips shut. He had, indeed, been about to tell Shane Tremant that Eva was amazing at her job and his ass was in more trouble than he realized. Sam was right, though; his mouth had caused him more than enough trouble already.

Neal raked his fingers through his hair. "Shane. Do you honestly believe a PI wouldn't have a cloud-drive backup of her files?"

Shane looked at Neal and then at Joshua and Sam.

"Erase them."

"How would we know how to get to her cloud drive?" Josh said.

The tension in the condo elevated as Shane seemed to ponder his answer. Reaching behind his back, he pulled a gun. Sam squealed, Josh tensed, and Neal cursed.

"Put that down, Shane," Neal insisted.

Josh held his hands up. "Listen to your friend."

"You." Shane used the gun to gesture at Sam. "Erase the files."

"She doesn't have Eva's password," Josh answered for her. "The only person who does is the head of the company."

Shane cursed, paced a few times, and then turned the gun on Neal. "This is your fault. If you hadn't hired her..."

The door opened, and Eva stopped just inside the condo. Her eyes darted around, clearly taking note of the situation. She barely moved her mouth but seemed to say something and then stepped in, leaving the door open. "What's going on, guys?" She kept her attention on Shane, not even acknowledging Josh and Sam, as she slowly eased forward.

"You're going to erase your files," Shane ordered. "Whatever you've got on me."

"Why would I do that, Mr. Tremant?"

He aimed the gun at Josh. "I'll kill him."

"And go to prison for murder?"

Josh didn't know how she was keeping her cool. He was starting to sweat as his heart rate increased at the constant pumping of adrenaline through his veins. His fight-or-flight instincts were definitely telling him to grab Eva and Sam and run, but he forced his feet to stay grounded.

Let Eva do her job, Joshua.

"You've got several witnesses here," she told Tremant. "You going to kill us all? And do what with the bodies? And the evidence trail? You really think nobody else has seen what I have on you, Shane? The ball is already rolling. All you're doing now is making things worse. Why don't you put the gun down and have a seat? I'll tell you everything we know." She'd continued moving closer until she had effectively placed herself between Shane and Josh and Sam.

Josh hadn't even realized what she was doing until it was too late. If Shane pulled the trigger, Eva was taking the bullet. Un-fucking-acceptable. He started to move, but Sam grabbed his shirt.

"Don't interfere," Sam whispered. "You could spook him."

"*We?*" Shane looked beyond her and let out a flat laugh. "Don't tell me that pussy is your partner."

"No. He's not. He's just an asset. I have an entire team that I report to, Mr. Tremant. Every bit of evidence I have, *they* have. You can kill us all. You still won't get away with embezzling from the HOA."

Shane's jaw tensed. "I'm not going to jail."

"Holding three people hostage isn't the best way to reach that goal."

"I'm not holding anyone hostage."

"Oh, so we can go," she said.

He lifted the gun. "Don't you fucking move."

Josh started to move forward, to get Eva out of harm's way, but Sam tightened her hold on his shirt.

"Don't move. She's working him."

"So you *are* holding us hostage, then?" Eva lifted her hands and moved closer to him. "That's bad planning, Shane."

"Just delete what you have on me."

"I told you. That won't matter."

The panic on his face was obvious. He was trying to

figure out his next step, but as always, Eva was two steps ahead. Shane reached up with his free hand, dragging his fingers through his hair. As he did, his attention was no longer on the gun aimed at Eva. Just a split second of obvious distraction, and she was on him.

Josh jumped, surprised at how fast she moved, like a cat attacking her prey. Eva closed the distance, slapped her hands—one on Tremant's wrist and the other on the gun—and had the weapon aimed at Tremant's head in the blink of an eye.

Shane screamed, clutched his hand, and looked up at Eva, stunned. Confused. His mouth sagged as she aimed the gun with far more confidence than he ever had.

"What the fuck?" He stepped forward, and she lifted the gun.

"Don't," she warned.

He started to call her bluff, started to move. Silently dared her to shoot.

"I kicked your ass once today. You really going to make me do it again?"

"I'm not going to jail," Shane insisted.

"Yeah," Eva answered. "You are."

Josh's stomach tightened. He didn't want to see Shane Tremant die, but if he took one more step toward Eva, Josh would kill the prick himself. Stepping forward, pulling his shirt out of Sam's grasp, he let out a breath of fire without even trying. He was enraged by the threatening look on Shane's face.

"Shane," he said, his voice unexpectedly calm. "I suggest you back away from my woman."

"Your woman?" He smirked as he looked at Josh. "You can't handle a woman like this. Me, on the other hand..." He made a show of looking Eva over, top to bottom, before licking his lips.

Josh ground his teeth and took a step forward, but he didn't have a chance to let loose on Tremant. Eva kicked Shane in the knee, his groin, and then his face. She shoved him to the floor and pressed her knee to his back. She pointed his gun at the floor next to his face, making sure he saw how close the barrel was to his head.

"You, on the other hand," she muttered, "are going to make some prisoner very happy."

"Police! Do not move!"

Josh cried out, "Stop! She's the good guy!" He lifted his hands high, showing he was unarmed but determined to prevent Eva from getting shot.

They ignored him. "Drop the gun."

Eva did as told, tossing the gun in her hand out of Tremant's reach, and then held her hands up. "I'm a private investigator. I have a loaded weapon on my right hip."

She kneeled, knee in Tremant's spine, while one of the officers patted her down, removing her weapon and gathering Tremant's before backing off.

Josh started to protest when the officer put cuffs on Eva, but again Sam reassured him that it was fine. Once they knew she wasn't a danger, they'd release her.

Tremant was cuffed next. Neal, the prick, stood there without any threat of being arrested; at least not yet.

Once Eva got done telling the cops what she knew and handed over all the evidence she'd gathered during the last week, that would change. Looking at the two men, Josh felt a swell of pride. She'd stopped them. In just a few short days, she'd caught them embezzling, cheating, and manipulating. And she was about to expose it all.

Catching her gaze, he smiled and mouthed, *You okay?*

She nodded. *You?*

Their silent conversation ended when a police officer approached Josh and Sam, ready to ask them what they had witnessed.

Eva accepted the round of "good work" and "nice job" that her team always handed out when one of them wrapped up a case. They weren't simply words and obligatory pats on the back. Each member of HEARTS knew how tough this job could be; even the cases that were more easily wrapped up than the Jupiter Heights Voyeur case deserved sincere accolades.

Her report had run a gamut of issues from the embezzlement conducted by Neal Price to the illegal video surveillance by Melly Donahue, as well as Melly's assault on Josh to steal his keys.

She insisted it had been her boyfriend's idea to make the videos public on the Web. He thought it was only fair to make a few bucks off the Tremants since they had gone to such great lengths to try to manipulate Melly into joining their little sex ring. Neal might have been trying to blackmail his way out of the sex ring, but his knowledge of the activities happening in the condo landed him in jail as well.

Eva didn't necessarily disagree that they deserved to have some kind of payback, but revenge porn was never a good thing. Ever.

The karma Courtney was facing was much more to Eva's liking. While she couldn't be arrested for her actions, her name and photo would likely appear in the news stories over the next few weeks as more details became available to the media. She might not spend a day in jail for trying to recruit lovers for herself and the Tremants, but she certainly would face public ridicule.

Brenda and Cody had been cleared of any wrongdoing, but Neal and Shane had been arrested for their part in stealing from the HOA. Melly was sitting in jail as well. For now.

She'd been smart with her actions. There were no clear images of her on the cameras she'd planted. Shane's shitty security hadn't kept any footage long enough to pinpoint that the person hiding the cameras had come out of Melly's condo, and the website was in Neal Price's name. Even though Cody insisted Melly had paid her, she'd done so in cash, so there was no proof beyond Cody's word.

A good attorney could probably get her out of serving any time for her crimes, but that wasn't for Eva to worry about. She'd accomplished what she had been hired to do. She'd caught the Jupiter Heights Voyeur and so much more.

"You okay?" Sam asked.

Eva nodded. "Yeah."

"Just so you know, Josh was really great today. He never once hesitated in making sure I was safe."

"Good. I'm glad."

"He was worried about you, too."

Eva nodded. She didn't want to think about how her heart had sunk to the pit of her stomach when she'd walked in and found Shane aiming a gun at Josh and Sam. She'd whispered over her shoulder to Brenda to call the police, and then her instincts had taken over. The only thing she cared about was getting Josh and Sam out of danger. Mostly Josh. Sam knew better than to do anything rash or stupid that could get her shot, but Josh?

She was terrified he'd taunt Shane or try to protect her and get himself hurt. But he'd done just what she'd rammed into his brain. He'd stayed calm and let her handle it. She'd say that was progress. If she had to.

"He feels really bad about what happened in the gym, Eva."

"I know."

"So. Maybe tell him you forgive him."

Eva narrowed her eyes at Sam. "You do realize that if he hadn't run his mouth, Shane Tremant never would have pulled a gun on you two, right?"

"I know. So does Josh. And he's beating himself up pretty hard about it." Sam lifted her brows, as if she expected some big reaction from Eva. "He's at the condo right now. Packing up his things. Maybe you should go pack up yours, too. You know, since the case is over and you can finally be rid of your unwanted roommate."

Eva drew a deep breath. "One of these days, that cute little grin of yours won't be enough to stop me from bashing your face in."

Sam's smile widened as she batted her eyes. "But that day isn't today. Seriously, Eva, go. Let him off the hook."

"Fine," she groaned under her breath as she rolled her head back. "Are you sure you're okay?"

"I am. Thanks to Joshua."

Eva stepped around the little instigator and grabbed her bag off the table. "Night, ladies," she called out as she headed for the door. She was met with a chorus of "good nights" as she headed to her car.

She had a million things rolling through her mind as she headed toward the condo, but by the time she arrived, her anger was gone. Yes, Josh had done something stupid. He'd let his mouth get away from him and endangered her case, but she knew he hadn't done it on purpose. He wasn't meant for this kind of work, and she'd known it. So had Holly and Alexa.

They never should have allowed him to join on this case. *She* never should have allowed it. Lesson learned all around. Several lessons. First, Josh needed to take some self-defense classes. Second, they'd never let an untrained person insert themselves into another HEARTS case. Third...third, she loved Joshua so much that the idea of losing him terrified her in ways nothing else ever had, and she'd do whatever she had to do to make sure that never happened.

Josh didn't feel right leaving the condo. Not when he and Eva hadn't set things right. Zipping his bag, he tossed it on the bed and looked around the bedroom. This was definitely not how he had expected his week to go, but he didn't regret one moment of helping Eva with her case.

He'd needed this time with her, living in her world, to really appreciate everything she'd always told him. He might be booksmart, he might know more things than most people, but he had been so wrong about Eva's job. Not only could she take care of herself, but she could take care of anyone else she needed to as well.

Seeing her in action had been thrilling and terrifying all at once. Her training in Krav Maga had saved him at least twice this week, and her intelligence had saved a lot more people from being further manipulated by Price and the Tremants.

Stupid that it had taken being put in this situation for him to fully appreciate all she had to offer. He should have done that from day one.

"Stop."

He turned, and his heart rolled in his chest at the sight of her standing in the bedroom doorway. "Stop what?"

She pointed to his head. She always did that when he

was overthinking. "Obsessing about what happened today."

"I screwed up."

She nodded. "Yeah, you did. So don't do it again, okay?"

"Never."

Coming into the room, she stood just in front of him. "It was my fault, Josh."

"I opened my mouth."

"I never should have let you—"

"Don't, Eva. I wanted to be here. I *needed* to be here."

"You could have been hurt."

He wanted to put his hands on her hips, but he clenched them at his side instead. He wasn't sure if she'd be okay with him touching her. "Yes, I could have been."

"I don't regret you being here, though," she whispered. "I'm glad we were able to work things out."

"You are?"

She nodded, and he couldn't stop himself from smiling.

"You're not breaking up with me over this?"

Laughing, she grabbed his shirt and pulled him closer. "I should kick your ass. But I'm not breaking up with you."

"Thank God," he breathed as he wrapped her in his arms. "I was so worried."

"I'm sorry." Hugging him back, she buried her face in his chest. "I was mad about the case blowing up. I didn't handle it well."

He laughed. "I didn't handle any of this well."

Leaning back, he ran his hand over her hair. "I'm not built to operate under constant pressure like this."

"I know you're not. And that's okay." Pressing her lips to his, she kissed him lightly. "I'll never put you in this position again."

"Please don't." He was sincere in his plea but also couldn't stop himself from smiling. "You're a fucking badass, Eva Thompson."

"I've been telling you that, Joshua Simmons."

Smiling, he pulled her against him. "You know, I was thinking."

"About?"

"About this house we're going to buy."

She brushed her hands up his chest and wrapped them around his neck. "What about it?"

Sliding his hands lower, he cupped her thighs and lifted her off her feet. Her legs tightened around his hips, and her feet locked behind him. "Well, I think we need that big jet tub we were talking about *and* a closet big enough for all the stilettos I'm going to buy you."

Her smile widened as he carried her to the bed and eased her down. "As well as a place to keep all the gimp masks I'm going to buy you."

"Don't forget my studded collar."

"Oh, baby, don't you worry about that."

THE END

CONTINUE HEARTS SERIES WITH STOLEN HEARTS

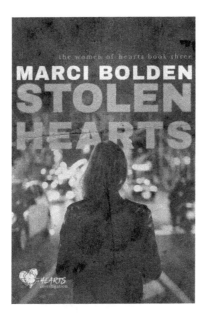

The Women of HEARTS Series Book Three

Alexa Rodriguez had spent the last twelve years obsessing about the night that her older sister had disappeared. Lanie had been there one minute. The next, she'd vanished. *Poof.* She was never seen again. The questions surrounding her kidnapping had never been answered. Hope that they ever would be had long ago evaporated.

Just like any traces of Lanie.

Alexa spent so much of her teen years learning how to work missing persons cases that she hadn't considered any career other than becoming a private investigator. She didn't want to be a cop, or a federal agent, or the teacher her *abuela* had tried to convince her to become. Her grandmother preferred she do something "safe," but Alexa had been preparing for solving cases most of her life. Even so, cases like the one unfolding before her had a way of shaking her core.

"She wouldn't have left without telling me." Dean Campbell had said those exact words at least four times since sitting at the table in the HEARTS Investigations conference room. "My little sister is in trouble."

"We believe you," Alexa said in a soothing tone she'd learned from her abuela.

Dean met Alexa's gaze and the desperation in his light brown eyes broke her heart. He scowled, causing the lines around his mouth to deepen, aging him before her eyes. He was no older than thirty, but the crease between his brows had yet to ease and he had a seemingly permanent frown on his thin lips. His shaggy hair was unkempt in a way that she didn't think was usual for him. He had dragged his fingers through the brown strands enough in the last fifteen minutes for her to recognize it as a nervous habit. He was genuinely distressed. So, yes, Alexa believed that *he* believed his sister was in trouble. She'd have to confirm that before *she* believed it, but his conviction was enough for her to want to comfort him.

Holly Austin, lead investigator for HEARTS, stared at Alexa in that way she always did whenever she worried about a case hitting too close to home for one of her teammates. Holly didn't think Alexa working missing persons cases was healthy, but at the same time, Alexa was the best one for the job.

"What do you think?" Holly asked pointedly. She wasn't asking what Alexa thought of the case. She was asking if Alexa was up for taking the case. Holly was the lead investigator for a reason. Not only because she was brilliant and strong enough to shoulder the weight, but because—whether she wanted to be or not—she was the most in tune with the others on her team.

Alexa loved that Holly always took the time to think before agreeing to take on a case. She might not be good a verbalizing how much she cared about her team, but she showed it every day in the way she looked out for them in little ways.

Dean sat across the table, his dark eyes moving from one PI to the other. "Is there a problem?"

Shaking her head, Alexa offered him a warm smile. While Holly's talent was assessing if one of her teammates was up for a case, Alexa's strength was reassuring their clients. "No. No problem. We're going to do everything we can to help you find Mandy. You'll be working directly with me, but my team will be kept informed on the case to make sure I don't overlook anything. I can't make you any promises, Dean, other than that every one of us will be dedicated to bringing your sister home."

Relief wasn't exactly the look on his face, but hope seemed to light in his eyes. "The police won't do a damn thing."

"She's nineteen, legally an adult," Alexa said. "Unless there's reason to believe she has been hurt or left against her will, there isn't much they can do."

"She might be an adult, but I still take care of her. I pay her living expenses so she can focus on school. I haven't heard from her for a *month*. She wouldn't leave without telling me. I'm her brother, for God's sake." Raking his fingers through his brown hair, he didn't notice —or maybe he didn't care—that the strands were now standing on end. "Do you think she left against her will?"

"We're going to find out."

As a teen, Marci Bolden skipped over young adult books and jumped right into reading romance novels. She never left.

Marci lives in the Midwest with her husband, kiddos, and numerous rescue pets. If she had an ounce of willpower, Marci would embrace healthy living, but until cupcakes and wine are no longer available at the local market, she will appease her guilt by reading self-help books and promising to join a gym "soon."

Visit her here:
www.marcibolden.com

facebook.com/MarciBoldenAuthor

twitter.com/BoldenMarci

instagram.com/marciboldenauthor